Hunger Eats a Man

HUNGER EATS A MAN

Nkosinathi Sithole

PENGUIN BOOKS

First published by Penguin Books (South Africa) (Pty) Ltd, 2015
A Penguin Random House company

Registered Offices: Block D, Rosebank Office Park, 181 Jan Smuts Avenue,
Parktown North, Johannesburg 2193, South Africa

www.penguinbooks.co.za

ISBN 978-0-14-353896-7
eISBN 978-0-14-353144-9

Text design and typesetting by Triexie Smit in 12/16 pt Minion Pro
Cover design by Michiel Botha
Cover photograph by Gallo Images
Printed and bound by CTP Printers, Cape Town

MIX
Paper from
responsible sources
FSC
www.fsc.org   FSC™ C017578

For Phiwa and Cebo

1

"The only thing that moves here in Ndlalidlindoda is time. Everything else is stagnant," Priest says to himself as he contemplates the land that has been his home for more than twenty years. It is now winter, and Priest hates winter. Gxumani, of which Ndlalidlindoda (Hunger-Eats-a-Man) is part, is situated near the Drakensberg mountains, so it gets very cold in winter. He has heard many people say that the City of Gold is cold, but he knows that no place can be colder than Gxumani, not in winter.

Yet Priest is now inured to the discomforts of cold. His only concern regarding winter is that the land loses its beauty. To him, the only thing that thrives in winter is the wind, and the wind makes him feel uncomfortable. Everything else is ugly and hungry. He focuses his gaze far away on the land owned by Wild Life and notices that the grass is dry and reddish white. Even the grass in his homestead seems to be crying for food. This prompts a thought in him that interests him so much that he wishes to share it with his wife. He goes inside and seats himself on the sofa.

MaDuma is fixated on the beadwork she is crafting to sell to the tourists at Zenzele (Do-It-Yourself). Priest spends a full minute studying the features of his wife. She is not really beautiful, but she is also far from ugly. MaDuma has lost almost all her back teeth and her cheeks are now sunken. However, this does not interfere with the fairness of her features. Priest thinks her eye-glasses make her look more beautiful than she actually is, then decides that this is unfair. But what is fair in this world any more?

Priest clears his throat and says, "I think here in Ndlalidlindoda it has been winter for many years now." He sounds excited by his observation.

MaDuma does not honour his introspection by raising her head as she answers, "You are hungry."

"Exactly! We all have been hungry for many years and that is winter."

MaDuma is greatly annoyed by her husband's asinine talk. She removes her eye-glasses and confronts him. "Get out!" she roars. "Don't bring your hunger to me. I've got my own problems!"

But later she calls him from where he is sitting outside and leaves a tray with his food on the coffee table. The food is served on a green-and-white plate and another identical one is used to cover it. Next to the covered plate his wife has placed a glass of water. Priest does not have to lift the covering plate to know that his food is pap and potatoes. For a long time now he has eaten pap and potatoes with his family. The taste of the food, or the absence of it, does not matter. It is better to have pap and potatoes than to have nothing.

As Priest is chewing his disagreeable food, he hears a soft voice speaking to him: "Father, the principal said we should bring R50 to school."

The voice is Sandile's, Priest's son of fifteen. He is, according to his father, a cute young boy who takes after him in being smart. Priest loves his son very much. But right now, just when he is hungry but cannot eat what is supposed to be his food, just when he is depressed, this boy tells him that he should miraculously have R50 to send to school. No! This is not his son!

He glances at the boy and sees a ghost or devil who has come to tempt him. Priest is angered by this devil in front of him. But his anger is contained when he recalls a day when, as a young boy, he was crying for food and his mother asked him if he thought that by giving birth to him, she could give birth to the food as well.

"He said they need the money to pay the privately paid teachers and the security guards," Sandile continues.

This makes Priest even angrier. The principal is now at the receiving end of his anger. The idiot! He will go to him right now! Priest looks at the ticking clock on the wall and decides that it is late, the principal will have gone home already. He seems ready to spit or swear, but then changes his mind when he sees the picture of Jesus hanging next to the clock, looking directly at him. For a moment he closes his eyes and says a short prayer. But his rage is too much for him, so he explodes, "This principal of yours is crazy! Where does he expect us to get the money from? Doesn't he know that there is no work? Even if we did have work, does he think we could give our money away to be wasted?"

Sandile looks at his father and thanks God that he does not have his black complexion. "But, Father—"

"No, my son. They will not eat my money. Let them do that to the fools."

As Priest finishes speaking, Sandile waits, confused. He is hoping that despite what his father has just said, he will tell him something meaningful to say to the teachers at school tomorrow.

Realising his son is not satisfied, Priest can only pledge to go himself to the school first thing in the morning. This will be a chance for him to spit out his anger. "Don't worry, son. I will tell the truth as I know it. They have to know that we know the truth."

Sandile becomes frightened.

"It took a brave man, son, to confront Shaka the king when he ruined his kingdom just because his mother had died. Sometimes the truth heals."

"Yes, Father, I understand." Sandile sounds as if he is going to cry.

The following day Priest awaits his children's departure for school before he prepares himself for his own errand. He looks content and pleased with himself as he puts on his priest's garb, which colours him all in black. The journey to school is a fifteen-minute walk from Priest's home. This is nothing to a man like Priest, who is used to walking. In no time he arrives at the school and heads for the principal's office, which is in the middle row of the three buildings that constitute Bambanani High School.

He knocks violently at the door and makes his grand entrance after he is invited in by a voice that disapproves of the way he has knocked. Seeing that it is Priest, the principal feels remorse for the way he has shouted at the representative of God and begins to apologise.

"I came here not as a priest but as a dissatisfied citizen. I came here as an unhappy taxpayer," Priest says in a voice the principal does not recognise.

The principal directs a surreptitious glance at the man in front of him and sees a priest all over. He sees an embodiment of the colour black. He sees Father Gumede. But who has just spoken to him? The principal looks again and realises there is nobody else. Whoever has spoken to him has used the respectable voice of Father Gumede. He tries to figure out what the matter is, but to no avail. So he decides to start from the beginning, as he knows it. "Good morning, Father Gumede."

"Yes, a good morning indeed, Mr Hadebe," Priest responds in a grim tone and the principal realises that, one way or the other, he has displeased the gods.

It pains the principal to consider what wrong he may have done. He can find no answer. He feels like someone who was too drunk the previous day to remember what wrong he might have committed. He soon understands that whatever the fault is, the only way to find it out is by asking Priest.

"Can I help you, Father Gumede?"

Priest is still busy trying to organise his words. There is too much to say and last night he did not sleep for trying to rehearse his speech. Now all his words have deserted him. But prepared or not prepared, he has to speak: "There is too much crime and unemployment is rife in this country. Why should common people suffer like this when those on top have everything? Hhe?"

The noise the children are making, the teachers loitering around not doing their work, all come between the two of them. The principal is frightened. His weak mind seems to have stopped working. But his memory is better, so he still recalls what Priest has said. "Yes, that is true. There is too much crime and many people are without employment." He feels inferior as he speaks.

"I happen to be one of those who are unemployed," Priest says triumphantly, as if being unemployed is the best thing that can befall any human being.

"Yes. Let's hope things will change for the better. It can't go on like this."

"This is not a matter of hope, Principal." Priest's voice is high. "It is too serious. Maybe you do not know that, because you are working and have money to take care of your family and yourself."

Priest's words hurt the principal. It is true: he has a good job and is able to support his family. He also knows that leading a healthy life among people who do not is sometimes viewed as some kind of weakness or betrayal. But what is he supposed to do? Must he quit his job and add to the statistics?

"Now, these children you are teaching here," Priest starts after a brief hiatus, "where are they likely to find employment?"

The principal wishes he could take this question as a rhetorical one, but it is not intended to be so. A look in the visitor's eyes tells him an answer is needed.

"You said you did not come here as a priest?"

"Yes. I'm nothing but a dissatisfied citizen."

"But still I want to ask you a question that may require your biblical knowledge." The principal does not give Priest a chance to respond.

"Do you think God loves everybody equally? The rich and the poor, the leaders and the led?"

Priest is taken aback by this question. He wants to leave God out of this. What does he know about God? What does he know about anything any more? Yet he cannot say that to the principal. So he decides to misunderstand the question. "Are you asking that because you are rich and I am poor?"

"No," the principal stammers, "I was just … I was just … asking." He wishes he could withdraw his words. "I'm sorry."

"Do you know how it is to be poor?" Priest shouts.

"You know," the principal starts sadly, "I am not very rich myself. I know how it feels when you want something and you cannot afford it."

"But you want us to pay for unnecessary things like the security guards and the privately paid teachers? Where do you think we will get the money from?"

Only now does the principal understand the reason for Priest's surprising and disturbing visit and, now that he is aware of the cause of his predicament, he begins to feel better. "The security guards and the privately paid teachers are very important, Father Gumede. There is a shortage of teachers and the government cannot afford to pay for all those we need." The principal feels strong again. He begins to feel the clothes he is wearing – something he ceased to do as soon as Priest came in.

"But how do you think we will pay if we do not have the money? Why don't you tell the poor souls to go home, plough the fields and wait for God to bring rain?"

The situation is tense in the principal's office. Priest is getting angrier and angrier, while the principal is now less afraid to speak his mind. This is Father Gumede, who knows nothing about how a school is managed.

"You were not in the meeting where we agreed about this. Now what do you want me to do?"

"I want you to tell me where am I supposed to get the money to throw into the water?"

"I think it's better for you to leave now, Father Gumede. We have wasted a lot of each other's time and it looks like our conversation is taking us nowhere."

"I'm not satisfied yet. I'm not leaving until I am satisfied. I am still as unhappy as when I came in here."

Priest's refusal to leave makes the principal realise he must take drastic measures if he is to free himself from this man who is so keen on torturing him. As he is busy thinking about the way out, the bell rings, marking the end of the current period and the beginning of the new one. The principal takes some papers and prepares to leave, intimating to Priest by a motion of his hand that he should do likewise.

Priest contemplates the practicality of refusing to go and decides it would be in vain. He stares straight into the eyes of the principal with such doggedness that the other man flinches. Priest is happy to see that. He is making his point.

"We are not finished yet!" he says grimly. "We will meet again, PRIN-CI-PAL!"

2

Priest strides proudly as he leaves Bambanani High School. He always feels important in his priestly garb, although his importance has receded before him like a dream. What concerns him most is that his children are now going through the pain he himself went through as he was growing up. For four years now his family has been struggling, living on the little money he got when he was retrenched from the bacon factory.

He started a spaza shop soon after the retrenchment, but within seven months he became aware that he was losing. Many people had no money to buy from him. When they bought on credit, they did not pay him back. Now his spaza shop has completely closed down. For the Gumede family, just getting something to eat is a struggle. This pains Priest very much. He swore to himself and others that, when he became a man, his children would not suffer like he had. This seemed to be true at the beginning, but now things have changed for the worse. His children are suffering and he does not know what they are thinking. They still respect him as a father, but the happiness with which they used to welcome him home is fading slowly.

As soon as his wife opens the door for him he starts talking, "Yes, that devil knows who I am now. I told him all I wanted to tell him."

"But you shouldn't have bullied the principal, Father. It's not his fault things are like this," MaDuma's voice is kind. This disturbs Priest, who knows his wife well.

"His fault or not his fault, I told him. Why does he want money from us when he knows we are starving?" Priest has taken off his trousers. Now he smiles as he removes the collar from his neck. "Besides, it's better to find a place to pour out your anger. I feel better now."

"I think you worry yourself too much about things you cannot change." MaDuma seats herself on the bed, getting even more serious and polite. "Everybody knows there is unemployment in this country."

The happiness that Priest felt when he came in diminishes. He feels a tinge of unease as he becomes aware that something serious is on his wife's mind.

"We need to be creative and find ways to make ends meet," MaDuma continues.

The troubled Priest looks back at his wife and asks in a voice of sadness and anger, "Like what?"

"They say Johnson is going to need people to work on the trees. It's not a great deal of money, but it can help."

"What?" Priest shouts. "No ways! I can't let my wife work on those trees. Like a slave on a farm? Tell me you are joking."

MaDuma's countenance changes as her husband utterly misunderstands her. "I was thinking that you should go," MaDuma's voice is stern, having decided to forsake her former politeness. "Other men work on the farms if they cannot find better jobs."

MaDuma has now stood up. She is pacing up and down the room. Priest feels like his head is going to explode. His wife continues, "It's better than staying at home and watching your children suffer."

"Work for nothing?" Priest is aghast. "It's better to work for nothing than to watch your children suffer? Is that what you are telling me?"

MaDuma decides to ignore the question. Instead, she heads for the door and says, "Think about what I said."

The door bangs.

Priest cannot help but think about what his wife has said, which is a pain in itself. He pledged to himself when he was a boy that he would never work on a farm again. He worked on one once and his experiences made him vow never to do it again, no matter what happened. Now his wife says he should break his vow? No. It is not the question of the vow. It's the reason he took that vow that matters.

Now that an old wound has been opened, Priest resolves to narrate his childhood story to his son. This may help the boy understand that the world has teeth with which it bites whomever it wants, whenever it wants. He seeks out the boy who is watching Oprah Winfrey's talk show. They are talking about a boy who died for forty-five hours and was resurrected. The boy in question started writing poems when he was about eight years old, just as old as Sandile was when he started.

Priest begins to narrate his story, even though his son's attention is not on him. "I'm telling you this so you will know that if you are suffering today, your suffering cannot compare with what we experienced. And since you are an aspiring writer, perhaps in my story you will find an idea for a novel, or a short story if your creative juices do not serve you well.

"But, as for me, I am telling you this so that I may come to terms with my past and feel better, if that is possible under the present circumstances. I hope to reduce, or even end my anger by this telling. They say that voicing your troubles is therapeutic. If that is true, then we both are going to benefit from this. My telling will heal my wounds of the past, and you will listen so that you can retell it and the story will then be yours and everybody's."

Priest spends an hour engaging with his past. Though it seems that Sandile is not listening, three days later he approaches his father with a short story he has written.

It is an ordinary day in December, and you are on holiday from school when you go out and see an unfamiliar tractor parked at the Ring. The Ring is the main stop at Skopo, where you live. It is where buses turn and it has therefore become circular, hence the Ring. When you see this tractor, you dash back to the rondavel, which functions as kitchen, dining room and bedroom. As you stand in front of your home, speechless, watching and wondering where this handsome tractor could have come from, news starts to circulate around the homesteads that the tractor is hunting for people to work at the farm. It is Mbaqa's tractor, people say, some eighty kilometres east of your place. School children who are on holiday are more than welcome to go.

You are uncertain whether you should join or not. The prospect of earning your own money is inviting, but you have a hunch that working there will not be a good idea. But when you hear that your friends, including your elder brother – who is two years your senior and looks as if he is your twin – are going, you decide to give it a try. You know you will be jealous if your friends have their money and you don't. Also, staying alone at home during the day would be worse than any hardship you may encounter at the farm. Only, you are wrong. Very wrong.

Thus, at about eight that morning, you find yourself at the back of the tractor – it carries a wagon that has steel walls but nothing on top – ready to be transported to the place you only know as Mbaqa. Mbaqa is a name black workers have given to the white farmer, and it has become his and his farm's name. Mbaqa! Even today that name causes memories of hardship: toiling, rain, sun, thunder, lightning. And fear. The fear of what you might be made to do. The fear of being entirely at the mercy of your employer. Baas.

One can say that going to the farm is some kind of an adventure for the four of you: you, your brother and your two friends. You have heeded Mbaqa's call for manpower, knowing that much may happen in that place. It is not hunger or poverty that has forced you to board the wagon. No. You go there because you fear jealousy when your friends get paid. You don't want to be left behind.

The tractor swings its way past Wonela and Entabeni farms, moving at high speed. It is moving too swiftly for a tractor. You have only known the old, sluggish tractors that some people in your village own, so you are fascinated by the speed of Mbaqa's tractor. It sounds like it has an engine as smooth as a car's. As the tractor speeds along, the wind hitting your faces and ears, you think about your past and your future. Who are you? A twelve-year-old boy on a tractor ready to offer himself to work for a white farmer. *Umlungu*. You are travelling on the tractor of someone you do not know, to a place you do not know. When you pass the huge dam belonging to Jesus's farm, you begin to have second thoughts. A voice inside you says, "You have made a grave mistake, you should not have come here." But there is no going back. The wind blowing past your faces is stronger as you reach Jesus's farm. It feels as though you have been kidnapped. You think that if you had the chance, you would escape, jump off. But there is none.

Even though part of you has been wishing that you won't be employed at the farm, you are. All of you. It is harvest time and the farmer needs as much cheap labour as he can possibly get. There are loads of potatoes to be picked and expanded fields to be cleared of potato plants. In no time a smaller tractor transports you to the fields where you are to work. There are people who have been consigned to other sections of the farm. The lucky ones are those who work in the shed. Working in the shed is the best thing that can happen to a Mbaqa farmworker; the work is not so bad there.

The first job you do in the fields is to remove potato plants so that the reaping machine does not get damaged. Can you believe that? You have to have your hands blistered in order to protect those lifeless machines. But a voice inside you says, "They are not really lifeless because they can move and make a good deal of noise. The machines do a great job digging those potatoes. Had they not been here to dig them, you would have to dig them with hoes that would also blister your hands." That voice inside you carries on talking. It tells you that you would have earned more money hoeing out potatoes in the vast fields. But that is not true. You do not even know how much you are to be paid for the work you are doing now.

Yes, it was foolish of you to rush to the fields without knowing how much you are going to be paid, but there is one important thing you know about the South Africa of the 1960s – it is not easy to talk to a white person. You are growing up with your fathers telling you a white man is your God, and nothing happens to disprove that. They have everything and you have nothing. There you are on such a big piece of land owned by one man. You live with thousands of people on land not even half as big. You are there to reap God-knows-how-many hectares of potato fields for the benefit of the white man. So it is easy to believe the white man is some form of a god. He is the owner of land and money and everything. The owner of lives. Your lives.

But it is the size of the fields that affects you most. Seeing all those rows of maize and potatoes, it feels as though you have arrived at some place beyond this planet. They stretch without end. The maize plants stand tall and green as you pass them on the way to the potato field, looking as though they are the ones that are moving while you stand motionless. So much food and you are hungry all the time!

This makes you think about the hunger you have left at home. Hunger is one thing you find yourself unable to deal with. As you are growing up, it seems to you that you are the weakest child when it comes to bearing with hunger. You are fascinated by the way your brothers and sisters are able to tolerate it. You remember a day when you were crying for food and your mother shouted at you.

"Why are you crying?" she demanded in a strangely harsh voice.

"I'm hungry," you told her.

Then she said something … You don't know if you should say it was strange or surprising or horrible. She said: "Now what do you want me to do? Do you think because I gave birth to you I can give birth to the food as well?"

You did not stop crying. You cannot tell what you felt about this. But you still remember those words clearly. All you know is that it hurt her very much to see you cry like you were doing, knowing she could do nothing to help you.

Your mother sometimes tells you to save your tears for when your father comes home from where he is working. It is in a factory in town where he lives in a hostel. He cannot afford the bus fare every day and they work shifts, sometimes starting work at two in the afternoon to ten at night. You hear they earn what is called *upondo nofishi* (pound and a fish). It is actually R2.50, and that R2.50 is not enough to support you. There are many of you. Too many even for someone who earns a better salary. That is why you vowed never to have more than five children, and you are glad that you have only two.

As a boy continuously haunted by hunger, it feels like a fair thing to blame your father. Your mother makes you believe it is your father's fault that you are starving. And your father, for his part, wants you to believe it is not his fault. That you are all victims. But you are not at your home now. You are at the fields of Mbaqa's farm. The fields have made you bitter and envious because of the hunger back home. Hunger! What a word if one really knows what it means!

On your first day of working you encounter another setback. As you know nothing about farms and farm labour, you forget that there will come a time for you to eat. You have nothing to put your food in. You spend most of your lunch time looking at people eating their food. The food is provided by the farmer, so it is not delicious at all. But you still want it because you are hungry. The cook sees that you have not eaten and serves you your food on the plastic bag she has with her. It is dry pap and sugar. Your hands are not just dirty, they are filthy. You have no spoon to eat with so you have to use those filthy hands, yet you do not hesitate. You devour your food as if nothing is wrong. One can say you have become like a pig. That's what farm work does to you sometimes, it makes you look and think like a pig.

You are about to finish when Zuma, the induna, shouts, "Dinner is over!"

You leave the plastic bag, which has the last of your food. You go to work only half content, complaining that Zuma should have let you finish your meal. But unfortunately Zuma does not permit anything he thinks would waste *umlungu's* money, as he keeps reminding all of you.

Zuma is the best overseer any farmer can hope for. He is loved by his employers and despised by his fellow workers. He is ugly inside and out. One of the few people you know who is endowed with complete darkness. Nobody ever speaks back to him. He beats people who dodge work. Then he reports them to the farmer, who will cut the person's wages. He hurls a potato at anyone who leaves it unpicked in their line. But he is most feared for his witchcrafting abilities. If you quarrel with him, you may lose your life in a mysterious manner. He watches and watches you for all the long hours that feel like days before the end of the shift strikes at five. "*Ishayile!*" Zuma announces.

You are fascinated by people's screams of celebration: "*Hhiyo!* It's it."

Your days at the farm are always tough. Not only is the work impossibly difficult, but natural forces also play their role in making your lives miserable. It is summer when you are at the farm. If it is not raining, it will be hot. You always suffer. But the days when it rains are always worse. The rain finds you in the fields and Zuma does not call off work until the word comes from Mbaqa or Sisusiyaduma (The-Stomach-is-Rumbling) that you should stop work and come to hide in the shed. The word always comes too late, when the rain is about to stop. Then you have to continue working in your miserable condition.

Today you are so drenched that your ticket is almost damaged. When you are ticketing, a white boy of sixteen looks at your ticket and you, "You see your ticket is like you?" This young man is Mbaqa's son. When he has said this to you he takes some time looking at your ticket, considering whether to sign it or not. He is known for refusing to sign those tickets that do not appeal to him. That means a person may have toiled in the farm the whole day for nothing. Others tease those people by saying that they worked the whole day for unpeeled potatoes, which are provided for lunch instead of sugar.

You are lucky; the young white boy signs your ticket. But you cannot help crying as you watch this boy: happy, dry and white! You have been working like an animal for him and his father, but instead of feeling sorry that you are drenched to the bone, he decides to mock you, and even contemplates punishing you. On the way home your fellow workers congratulate you that he signed your ticket, but you are crying. You keep looking at yourself and the ticket that is, indeed, as wet as you are.

So it is that you vow never to work for the white farmer again. The physical and emotional abuse you suffer is beyond words. You feel that just being in this place is abuse enough for you.

But it is at the end of your working period that the final blow is struck. It happens like this. At the end of each day the tractor transports you back to the offices for ticketing, when they log your hours of work. The three of you – you, your brother and Thami – earn eight cents a day while Tila earns seven cents. In fact, what happens is that you all ticketed seven cents the first day. But the following day Sisusiyaduma gives you a one-cent increase, changing the seven of the previous day to eight.

Trouble comes when you are supposed to get paid. It is a week before the end of the month when Mbaqa summons you to the shed even before you go to work. He tells you that the police are on their way to arrest you because you have fraudulently tampered with your tickets, offering yourselves more than you deserve. The thought of being in the police van is very scary to you, not to mention spending a night in jail. You are not alone in this feeling because, as the police arrive, all four of you are begging Mbaqa not to send you to jail. Mbaqa is now blood red with anger, telling all who can hear that he has nothing to talk to you about. You are criminals and in his book criminals need to be put away from society.

By this time Sisusiyaduma is pacing up and down, denying vehemently that he has increased your pay, but still begging Mbaqa not to dispatch you to jail. You believe these two are playing tricks on you. Why did Mbaqa not notice earlier that your payment has been increased? He has ticketed you himself many times before.

After pleading and begging, something disturbing happens. Mbaqa agrees to give you your money, without removing the extra one cent a day. Instead of having you arrested, he offers to pay you half of what you have worked for, or what you think you have worked for.

You are so grateful not to be arrested that you take the money. It is then that you realise the paradox of your lives. How can you be grateful when you have been toiling in the harshest of conditions for little money, and yet that little is cheated from you into even less?

Some people will think your story is not worth telling when all this mad exploitation is over. But you know your story is worthwhile. Without your story, your country will have no history. Or its history will be partial and untrue, as it has been.

3

On the Wednesday of Priest's visit, Bongani Hadebe leaves Bambanani High School – his school, as many people refer to it – tired and angry. He is short in height and has a big, protruding stomach that many people attribute to the large quantities of beer and brandy he gulps every day. He is very light in complexion and is known for his penchant for costly, beautiful clothes, such as Brentwood trousers, of which he has twenty pairs. He comes from a rich family, his father having once owned a number of stores and buses called Phuzushukela (Drink-Sugar), after his nickname. Wealth allowed Phuzushukela's son to become hooked on wearing costly clothes at a young age. Not only did he have all the kinds of clothes he wanted, he was also the only student to drive to school, when even some of the teachers didn't have cars. Students joked that Bongani could change cars while they could not even change shoes.

But Bongani is also known for his lack of intelligence and the fact that he reached his present position by buying his diploma certificate. Only God knows how he got his university degree.

Bongani climbs into his bottle-green Audi A6 and drives slowly out of the gates, absently saluting Mr Ndlovu, the security guard. He turns to his right when he joins Giants Castle Road, and Ndlovu notices his boss is not going home. Bongani wants to take time to clear his mind because he is worried by Priest's visit. More than that, he is mad at his wife, Nomsa, because she does not want him to be a man. Last night he fought and lost what he thought was his last battle and now he feels like screaming.

When he reaches the bridge at Ncibidwane, his ill mind urges him to let the car drive straight into the river, but "Not yet" says another part of him. He continues on, past Ncibidwane Clinic and the taxi rank and through MaHlutshini Village. He relishes the sight of the gorgeous Drakensberg mountains and feels some consolation in his heart. The big, dark rocks seem as if they might open up and allow him to meet the two beautiful characters of the fairy tale, Demane and Demazane.

He parks his car when he is about two kilometres from Giant's Castle and climbs the hill on foot. He knows the area now belongs to KZN Wildlife, but he decides that no one will arrest him since it is daytime and he has no dogs or hunting tools. As he walks, Bongani comes across a family of five baboons. "Even the ugliest animals have children and I don't!" he laments. As if they hear him, the baboons laugh and go on, seemingly heading for a small area called Place of Power.

Before Bongani is a big, dark forest. He is tempted to go back to the car, but looking down, he notices how his trousers and shoes are covered in dirt. That dirt, and some greater force, are pushing or pulling him towards the forest. This is where the bones of his great ancestor, Langalibalele, lie. It fascinates him that some people are so sacred that rather than being buried in graves dug for them, big rocks open up to take their dead bodies into themselves.

Just now he remembers a day two years before when all the Hadebe males gathered for the ritual of appointing the new chief. How much he had hoped and prayed that the ancestors would choose him! Perhaps if they had been living people he might have been able to influence them by speaking the most convincing language he knew – money. But dead people do things their own way. He had not liked that thin bastard Fana before that day, but his hatred towards him multiplied considerably when Fana turned out to be the chosen one. If he had not seen for himself the corn before everybody closed theirs in their hands, he would have said there was something sinister about the appointment. But each person held the corn for five minutes in front of the spectators and, when they opened their hands, Fana's was already sprouting.

"But why would the ancestors choose someone so thin instead of me? What do they see in someone who farts by the bone?" he demanded angrily when he was coming from the meeting. Now he forces this thought out of his mind.

Bongani feels tears form in his eyes as he contemplates his surrounds. This is the place where the great African who fought with the colonialists rests. It angers him to think that it was another African chief who finally conquered his great ancestor on behalf of the whites. "I hate Chunus!" he tells himself.

Again, he thinks about his warrior ancestor, and this time he feels ashamed of himself. Langalibalele was a brave man and he, his great-grandchild, is a coward! At thirty-seven he has no child of his own. Not because he cannot have them, but because his wife does not want to have children because, as she says, she is not a slave to bear children. Compounding his sorrow is his inability to let his wife know that he cannot be happy without having children. How can he be happy if even the baboons laugh at him?

He has seated himself on a rock now. At times he cannot stop the tears from dripping down his face as he meditates on his marriage. Why doesn't he leave her? The thought of living without Nomsa is as hurtful to Bongani as not having children. It is hard to think of replacing her with someone else. That is out of the question. Impossible. He just cannot live without his wife. But why doesn't she understand? Why doesn't she understand that he needs to be a man? He needs to leave his name on earth when he dies.

Bongani is gripped by a sudden fear. He feels his scalp tingle as he sees a tall, strongly built man standing just in front of him. He seems to be heavy with contempt, and this frightens Bongani even more. The man then speaks in a piercing voice and Bongani feels as if the whole world is supposed to hear it: "I am disappointed in you!"

The words enter through Bongani's ears and he thinks he may never be able to hear again. But he does, and wishes he has not.

"We left you to look after our homestead and you destroy it? Coward! How can you let a woman rule our homestead? Hhe? Don't you see that you will kill our homestead if you let that woman of yours lead you astray? Have you ever heard of a Hlubi whose wife hauls him around by the nose?"

The anger in the man seems to be the cause of the cold air that Bongani feels and breathes. He feels so cold that he thinks he may freeze to death.

"I say," the man continues, "if you are incapable of running our household, I will kill you!" At these last words the man plunges his spear into the ground and it comes out red with blood. "A man is a man thanks to his children!" the man says, as if in conclusion, and disappears from Bongani's view.

Bongani stands up and turns around twice. He sees there is nothing around him, but it feels as if something dangerous is looking at him. He jumps and cries, "Oh! My mother!" when he hears the baboons laughing not very far from him. He runs down to his car and the baboons laugh louder now, their voices enhanced by the mountains, which also sound as if they are laughing at him. Bongani locks himself in the car and tries many times to start it without success. He is trembling and trying to get that vision out of his mind. Was he dreaming up there or was what he saw a visitation? What he knows for sure is that, either way, he has seen a man who is certainly his ancestor. The message is that his ancestor wants him to give birth to many Hlubi boys who will also give birth to yet more Hlubi boys when they grow up.

Realising his ancestor's command is the same as his own wish, Bongani is happy. Only now is he able to start his car, reverse it and turn back home. He drives a little faster when he looks at his wristwatch and sees that he has spent more time in the mountains than he thought he would. But now he has more courage to continue with the struggle for his manly right, knowing that his ancestors support him. He needs children and he is going to have them. No wife of his – yes, of *his* – will deny him the privilege of having children. Never!

All these years he has been trying to reason with his wife that they should at least have two children, a boy and a girl, if possible. He cannot forget that every time he has tried to speak to her about this, she asks him whether he married her because he loves her or because he wants to procreate. Now that she has deprived him for so long, he wants to have ten children: seven boys and three girls. Yes. He wants ten children, at least ten children. His great ancestor will be pleased with him when he has fathered so many Hlubi boys who will continue the Hlubi line. He can see in his mind's eye a number of cute, healthy boys who precede each other by only a year. Yes. Because Nomsa has deprived him of the joys of fatherhood for so long, she is now going to bear him a child every other year. The good thing is that he is working and earning a lot of money through his other position in the Bambudonga (Catch-the-Wall) Regional Council. What is the use of having a lot of money if you do not have children to spend it on?

It is half past six now as Bongani arrives home. He parks his car in his garage and notices that the 4x4, as they refer to Nomsa's car, is parked outside its garage. He takes some time, admiring his huge and beautiful double-storey house. Who else but him in Gxumani has a house with stairs?

The place name, Gxumani, is the diligent work of the Rainbow Nation. It refers to what used to be two mutually exclusive areas. The one is Canaan, formerly a suburb designated as Whites Only during the years of Separate Development. Now it has been usurped by rich blacks like himself, while many whites have left to live in the other, even more expensive, parts of town where blacks cannot yet afford to buy. Ndlalidlindoda began as an informal settlement, but now many people have built houses as big as eight rooms and more, while others prefer to emulate the structure of their rural homelands by building up to three houses, some of which are rondavels and others called "kneel-and-pray". But none can compare with the houses in Canaan, and certainly none are as beautiful as his. So the best thing to say is that there is no house in Canaan as costly as his, thanks to his fine job as a principal and finer one as chancellor in the Bambudonga Regional Council. This makes him proud.

Now no one goes to Gxumani without noticing or hearing of Bongani Hadebe, the rich man. His home has become a landmark in Canaan, which people use to direct their relatives. "Tell the driver that you will alight at The Stairs!" people will tell others, to Bongani's delight. "At The Stairs!" those who take the taxis in his street say if they want to get off. All this makes Bongani happy, but it is always spoiled by the fact that he does not have children. He feels that not having children reduces him to the level of the common people. These poor people do not have a beautiful house and a lot of money like him, but he also does not have children like them. It feels as if what they have is stronger and more valuable than what he has.

"My uncle is a policeman!" one of his friends used to boast when they were growing up, and Bongani always beat him by saying, "My uncle is a chief!" Now he can only say, "I have a double-storey," and someone can reply, "I have five kids!" But all this is going to change. He can't help feeling grateful as he looks at his spacious home and sees many children playing and fighting in it. He can see himself teaching his boys to play ball and to ride bicycles. He feels as if he is a new person as he enters through the front door, until he remembers that Nomsa will be mad at him for not coming back from work on time. He suffers a little pang of fear as he notices that his wife is not only cleaning the house, but she is sweating as she cleans.

4

Nomsa arrives home at exactly half past four in the afternoon and expects to find her husband home as usual. She expects him to welcome her in with a kiss and then ask her if he can make her a cup of coffee. This is almost a habit now. A good one, at that. She braces herself for the love her husband will pour on her and is greatly disappointed when she realises there is nobody home. Her husband has left school and gone to only God knows where. Anywhere but home!

She tries to recall if he told her of any meeting that might cause him to be late, but he told her nothing. A thought says, "Maybe something he had not planned for came up." Another negates it soon after, reminding her that Bongani knows the number at her office and he also has her mobile phone number.

Thinking of phones, when last did Bongani call her at work and tell her that he loves her so much, he wishes the day was over so he could go home to her, or she could come home to him? The answer to that question, which is "not lately", makes Nomsa breathe faster. She thinks about her age and decides that, at thirty-nine, she is not getting any younger. How many stories has she heard of teachers, especially principals, having affairs with girls in their schools? She gazes at the dressing-table mirror and does not like what she sees. Is she fat? "Not that much!" is the answer, and it is not too bad. Is she uglier than she used to be? She cannot enunciate a resounding "no" to this question, and wonders how many times Bongani has asked the same question. She decides she does not want to know the answer.

"The short swine is having an affair!" she announces to the room, and some unknown force makes her look again in the mirror. This time she displays her teeth and shoves her tongue through the gap and makes some odd noise as she forces air through it. That having been accomplished, she says, "Shi!", which she always says when she is displeased, and then starts to move about in the room. Her mind gallops as she tries to reach the woman who wants to take her man and make her a laughing stock. Perhaps it is someone she knows. Perhaps it is not. It really doesn't matter. What matters is that Bongani has something going on and he has betrayed himself today.

"Son of a bitch!" she yells at his photograph, and suddenly goes to look at the clock on the sideboard and sees with much distress that it is five minutes to five. Bongani could not have left school later than three. Maybe he did not go there at all? The thought of him spending the whole day with a young schoolgirl makes her want to scream. "I will kill him! I will kill him! I will kill him!" she sings.

It is as if she has gone mad. She makes some inaudible noise and breaks open Bongani's wardrobe, although the key is just in front of her. She removes all the things she can in the frenzy of her anger. She descends the stairs at a run, taking them two at a time, as if trying to make sure that nobody can stop her. She uses the back door to the little garden and makes a bonfire out of the items she is carrying. She is not a fool for Bongani to humiliate. What she has done to his clothes is nothing compared to what she is yet to do to the man himself.

It soon becomes clear to Nomsa that burning Bongani's things does not quench her anger as it has always done in the past. If only he would arrive so that she can teach him a lesson. She feels that the anger inside her is too much, and decides to call on her second anger-countering strategy: cleaning! She goes inside and performs what she calls "thorough cleaning". She works hard and fast so that she can sweat out the anger.

She has turned all the living-room furniture upside down when she hears Bongani's garage door open. She stops her cleaning and watches Bongani touch and caress a young girl in a blue skirt. The sight prompts her to balance the broom on her shoulder and then to hold her hair up with both hands, as if trying to take off and fly.

When Bongani finally comes in, Nomsa has already failed to stop herself from crying. She sees his trousers covered in dust and grass and screams so powerfully that the house seems to vibrate. She charges towards him with the broom and Bongani is taken by surprise. He is still thinking about his vision and his resolution to demand his manly right, so it takes some time for him to make sense of what is going on.

Nomsa is a powerfully built woman and always prides herself on being two inches taller than her husband. Both these qualities count in her favour now. Her anger affords her the power she never thought she possessed and she uses it efficiently. Bongani tries to take it like a man but soon accepts that Nomsa is a strong woman and she has a broomstick while he has nothing. He tries to parry her attacks with his hands, but they soon feel so hurt that he decides to stop protecting himself with them.

"*Awe malo!*" he screams. "I promise I won't do it again!"

It isn't easy to speak and be beaten at the same time, but he does a good job. Nomsa only realises what she is doing when she hears Bongani ask for forgiveness and she thinks she sees blood leaking from his head. Now Nomsa cries, not out of anger, but out of fear for what she has done and out of what feels like love for the man she has just beaten. She throws away the broom, lest she beats him again, and tries to touch him. But then she sees the blood. She isn't afraid of blood, and there is not a large quantity of it, but somehow she feels as if touching him would cause more harm.

"But why, Bongani?" she manages to say. Then, having assured herself that he is not going to break in her hands, she tries to help him up.

Bongani is still confused. He wishes he would wake up from this nightmare, but he does not. Is this another dream or vision? No! If it was it wouldn't hurt this much. The fact is that his wife has beaten him. The good thing is that, although he certainly knows his wife is strong enough to beat him anyway, it consoles him that she has taken him by surprise.

"Why didn't you warn me that you were on the attack?"

Nomsa hears but cannot answer. She hurriedly goes to the bathroom, leaving Bongani on the misplaced sofa. She pours water in the basin and, as it is still pouring, she shakily searches the cabinet for Dettol or anything that she might use. As things fall from the cabinet, she suddenly recalls that there is a clinic nearby and stops the tap at once and runs for the living room.

"Let me take you to the clinic," she offers, and it feels pleasant that she can still think of something so helpful under such pressure.

Nomsa's words sound to Bongani as if she wants to display to the whole clinic community that she has beaten her husband. "No ways! I'm not going there. I'm fine."

"No, Bongani, you are not! Let me take you to the clinic so that they will stitch your head."

"Let me take you to the clinic so that everybody will see that I beat you up!" is what Bongani hears. "Hell, no!" he shouts. "I said I'm fine. I'm okay, okay?"

"All right." Nomsa is calmer now. "Please don't shout. I was just trying to help." She begins to cry again. Only now does she consider her reason for beating her husband. "Where were you, Bongani?" She wipes her tears with her left hand and looks closely at him.

"You should have asked that before you did this to me," Bongani contemplates his hands as he speaks and is frightened when he sees how swollen they are. "What difference will it make now? Hhe?"

"I said I'm sorry, Bongani. But I need to know why you did not come home to me. Why, Bongani?"

Nomsa seats herself next to him and it angers her that she is begging a man. She again sees blood on his head and she feels that she really loves him. Now she thinks about losing him and it makes her mind and body weak. Life would be sour without him. Where in this crazy patriarchal world would she find a husband as understanding as Bongani, who is able to bear with her unwillingness to have children?

"I'm serious, Bongani. Where were you all the time after you left school?" Nomsa is softer now, but she still speaks in a worried tone. Bongani is touched, but he does not want to answer her. Where was he anyway?

"Do you have a girlfriend, Bongani?"

Bongani tries without success to stop himself from laughing. "What do you say? Is that a joke?"

Before they go to bed, Nomsa has long forgotten about the "little incident", as she now thinks of her beating of Bongani. He pretends that it is all over for him too. But, as Nomsa relates to him how her meeting that afternoon went, he keeps reliving the pain and confusion he felt when she beat him. Thanks to his role-playing ability, she is honestly convinced and gratified that her husband has not only forgiven her, but has completely forgotten about the beating.

"Remember that we African women were doubly oppressed," she says about the meeting. "We were oppressed as black people and also oppressed as women. Now we have attained our freedom as blacks, but our struggle as women continues." She takes a heavy, long breath. "And we intend to win!"

Suddenly she leaves the room as if she fears something deadly is lurking. Bongani thinks about the days when he was growing up. His mother told him that if he was in the room with the cat and there was thunder and lightning, if the cat dashes out of the room he should follow it. It means there is danger. Now he smiles as he decides that if there was lightning and Nomsa was the cat, he would not follow her. He is not young any more. But he knows that his wife left because she is on the verge of crying. It amazes him how Nomsa is so touched by the cause of women. Every time they speak about the plight of women, she changes dramatically, getting more fearsome to Bongani.

"I wonder why she hates men so much?" he asks himself.

5

Priest knows that his wife is not absolutely wrong to consider the possibility of seeking work at the farm. It has become clear that he is unlikely to get a job anywhere else. Many people disapprove of farm work because of meagre wages and bad conditions there. "But things have changed now," he thinks. "Apartheid is gone and workers, including farm workers, have rights." But new laws or old ones, this is not the kind of work for a man as respectable as he is. Hasn't he been degraded enough? Even his priest's garb, the only suit he has left, is now threadbare. His shoes? He might as well have none, so worn are they.

His wife keeps pestering him about making a smart decision. Though the only smart decision to her mind is for Priest to decide to go to work at the farm.

"How much do you think Mr Johnson is going to pay us, or let me say, those who will work for him?" Priest asks her. He is beginning to give in to her persuasion. There is nothing very bright about farm work, but he tries to think positively about the money and the prospect of earning something, anything.

MaDuma realises she is winning him over. She is smart enough to understand that if she tells him the truth, he may be discouraged. So she almost doubles the money that she heard will be paid to tree workers: "It's not that bad. R30 per day."

Having received the answer, Priest looks fixedly at one spot, not winking or blinking. Then he says, "It's about six hundred a month. It's indeed worth a try. It's better than having to go begging."

"I'm glad you see that, Father. We and our children will not starve like this if you work there," MaDuma says with a sense of satisfaction. She has won her womanly battle of convincing the man to do the right thing.

Priest finally agrees that he will try his luck at the farm on Monday. During the weekend he spends a lot of time considering the decision he has made. He thinks that, despite everything, he has taken the right path. He thinks about the things he can do with R600 and realises how limited they are. But he will be staying at home, not having to pay for transport like he had to do when he was working at the bacon factory.

In the sermon on Sunday, he preaches about the importance of taking responsibility. This means doing all people can in order to fulfil their duties, no matter how much sacrifice is involved. He makes an example of the present situation where many people are without jobs, thus rendered unable to support their families and themselves.

"But if you wait and listen, if you keep quiet and think deeply, you will see that there is so much we can do. We should stop thinking too much about our grandeur and power, and consider what options we've got." He pauses for a moment and then continues, "Who can tell me that they have tried to seek work at the farms and were unsuccessful?"

When he poses this question, everybody nods their understanding. Everybody in the church today is moved by Priest's sermon. Many people reconsider their opinions about farm work and their present situations. Many listen and are touched, though some already have jobs. They feel the truth of what Priest says. It is not him who is talking to them, but it is God Himself. No mortal man can utter such words of wisdom without intervention from God. Some can even refer to the Bible: "At the beginning there was the Word. The Word was with God. The Word was God." Priest knows his way around words. This has contributed to his promotion from a mere churchgoer to his present position of priesthood.

Before dawn on Monday, MaDuma wakes up and prepares food for her husband to eat before going to the farm. She also packs lunch for him to eat if he is lucky to be employed. Priest, like everybody who knows farms and farm work, knows that he has to leave his household as early as possible. So by six o'clock he leaves and heads for Manhlanzini Stop where Johnson's truck is going to fetch them.

As he walks, he thinks he may be the first to arrive at the stop, but he is amazed to see that there are many people already waiting. Four hundred people at least, ranging from youngsters of thirteen to men and women of his age.

"Dear Son of God! Where are all these people coming from? Why aren't they seeking employment somewhere else?"

Priest considers the possibility of trying to hide the fact that he is going to the farm and realises that he cannot. His physical appearance – the old boots and a tattered creamy-white overall – testifies to his being prepared for farm work. His lunch box, carried in a Shoprite-Checkers plastic bag, tells everyone that Priest has food to eat at the farm.

Recognising the position he is in, Priest starts to blame himself for giving in to his wife's selfish demands. Almost all the people already waiting here at Manhlanzini Stop know Priest. He is a renowned man. They direct their gazes at him as he drags himself towards them. The sudden silence of those staring at Priest makes the others do the same. They want to find out what is going on.

The people standing at Manhlanzini Stop look so much alike that Priest cannot recognise any particular person, yet he knows that he is familiar with many of them. This makes it hard for him to choose his sitting position. He simply remains standing and gazes at the people with a confused and worried face. Some are whispering:

"The Priest!"

"Father Gumede!"

Some even go so far as to state the reason for their encounter with such an eminent personage: "Father Gumede is going to work on the trees with us."

Priest hears these words and sees the expectant looks of others. He does not know whether to greet everybody and sit down, or to sit down and greet only those who are seated next to him. But, somehow, he feels as if these people expect more than just a greeting from him. He wishes the truck would arrive right now and save him the humiliation.

"For how long must we suffer like this?" The words slip out of Priest's mouth as he puts his lunch box down next to him. There is something about Priest that makes people feel secure as they listen to him. The whispers that occurred earlier have ceased. All want to hear as Priest wrestles the Word from God. He has won it. It now belongs to him.

"Why is it that we should come here, as miserable as we are, to offer ourselves to work as slaves for the white man? Is this what we voted for?" Priest stops for a while, turns his head to observe his audience. He can tell by their serious countenances that his words have a profound influence on them. "What is R30 for the whole day of hard work and sweating?"

A certain woman from the seated group feels obliged to intervene when she hears Priest almost double their prospective earnings. "I think you are mistaken, Father. The money is R16. I heard from someone who heard from someone who heard from the white man himself."

Priest stops to listen to the woman who is offering her information. This greatly influences his temper and makes him run out of words. God has reclaimed His possession.

As Priest stands there, speechless and breathless, an argument commences regarding whom the people must believe. Priest has furnished them with good news, or better news, and the woman who negated his information is offering nothing but bad news. Those who are seated next to her look at her closely, trying to ascertain if her appearance qualifies her to contradict such a powerful person under any circumstances. The viewers decide that she is unattractive, notwithstanding her being prepared for farm work.

"She is ugly."

"No sane person can believe a woman who is ugly."

"An ugly woman is a foolish woman."

"She needs to be beaten."

A number of people are not angry at the woman because she has told them something they themselves have known. Many think that, no matter what they have known earlier, if Priest says they will earn R30, then it must be true. Somebody else might have made a mistake, but not Priest.

Priest is still speechless while people reorganise their thoughts. He looks awkwardly at them as his mind moves back and forth. In a few moments he counts how much they will get per month if they earn R16 per day. His finding troubles him so much that he pronounces it in a loud and worried tone, "R320 per month?"

Many people are confused when they hear Priest utter his finding. They do not know whether it refers to R30 or R16. But then the truck arrives and saves Priest from having to address them further.

6

Sithole, Priest's friend, refuses to seek employment at the farm. He is convinced that his ancestors have a far better job in store for him, so there is no need to sell himself to be a slave for a white farmer.

"Not in a million years!" he said boastfully to Priest on Saturday, when Priest was trying to convince him to go. Priest knew that he was fighting a losing battle, but spoke to him anyway for the sake of MaXulu, Sithole's wife, who begged him to talk some sense into her husband. They both knew, though, that nothing could change Sithole's mind if he had let himself believe his ancestors wished for him to follow a certain path.

"He is a hundred per cent believer in ancestors. It's astonishing," Priest always says.

Life is hard at Sithole's home, as it is in almost all the homes in Hunger-Eats-a-Man. Sithole has been without a job for six years now. He was working as a bus driver at Putco in Durban and used to get a good salary there, something both he and his wife came to realise when he lost the job. In those days his was counted as one of the well-to-do families in Hunger-Eats-a-Man, and he indeed "did not mind it", as he told his wife every time he got an opportunity. MaXulu's opinion on the matter – that her husband actually relished the thought of being among the wealthy men according to Hunger-Eats-a-Man standards – was closer to the truth.

The Sitholes have a five-roomed house, which qualifies as beautiful due to three facts: it is made of bricks, it is plastered, and it is painted. The creamy-white colour is now fading, but it does not deter Sithole's pride. Both he and his wife point to their home without fear or shame. When things were not yet like this, visitors were always encouraged, the aim being to show people how expensively and beautifully furnished the house was inside. But when hunger strikes, no one brags about wood and cloth, no matter how expensive.

Before Sithole lost his job, he was contemplating reroofing his house with tiles, something he correctly believed would have made him a force to be reckoned with, not only in Hunger-Eats-a-Man, but in the whole of Gxumani. But his dream did not come true because of the retrenchment. He came to realise there were many sacrifices he had to perform for his ancestors with the small amount of money that made up his retrenchment package. In the first three years after his retrenchment, Sithole slaughtered a goat every month and four cows a year on average. This made him a renowned and respected man in Ndlalidlindoda. Some young men, whom MaXulu detested with all her heart and called good-for-nothing trash, were so full of respect and admiration for Sithole that one of them, Kitoto, even seriously contemplated changing his surname to Sithole, something that gratified Sithole as much as it aggravated his wife.

There is also a rondavel in Sithole's homestead. It is neat and good-looking in spite of its age. It is only the thatching, which is eroded and black, that testifies to the fact that the rondavel has occupied the same space for more than fifteen years. It is also plastered and painted like the house. But the colour is white. MaXulu suggested it would make sense to paint it creamy white too, but Sithole insisted on a pure white colour because it symbolises good luck. In this view, he was supported by his ancestors, who visited him in a dream and told him that their house must be painted in white.

The rondavel is the most significant building in Sithole's homestead, according to him, at least. It is used solely for communication with the ancestors and for performing sacrifices to them. Sithole is one of the few men MaXulu knows who love and trust their dead relatives so much that they pray to them on a daily basis. Every evening, round about six, Sithole retreats to the rondavel, where he burns incense and talks to his ancestors about anything. "As if they care," MaXulu usually says to herself. It is only when Sithole makes sacrifices in the form of goats and cows, and when he thinks the subject he wants to consult his ancestors about is of particular importance, that he calls MaXulu and the children to be present and pay respect. This angers MaXulu, who sees no point in sitting there listening to someone talking to the wall.

The fact that Sithole does not want to go to the farm and try his luck like other men annoys MaXulu a great deal. She cannot even imagine some invisible spirits watching over them and making plans to better their lives by offering Sithole a job of his dreams, whatever that is. No. That is not going to happen, and Sithole knows it.

"Why didn't they do that in the last six years that you have been without a job?" As much as MaXulu respects and fears her husband, she just cannot keep quiet about this. "No, Sithole. Just say you are afraid of hard work at the farm. You got spoiled when you worked sitting down when you were a driver at Putco."

MaXulu is in a state of quandary. A part of her wants to threaten Sithole that if he does not go to seek work at the farm, she will. This she can say in spite of having been involved in a car accident that left her spine so fragile that she cannot do hard work. But now she knows her husband will gladly let her go. This thought increases her suspicion that her husband is afraid of hard work.

Thinking of hard work, why is it that men of today are so weak and lazy? MaXulu doesn't know. But she knows there was a time when men were men. When men were not afraid of sweating. She recalls, with great veneration, that her own father had resigned from his job when he was promoted – which sounded to him like a demotion – to work as a clerk in the office, instead of pushing wheelbarrows full of concrete and cement outdoors. He told his employers that he was unwilling to do such a feminine job, that he would rather go to seek work somewhere else. Some place where they would not insult him by giving him a job fit for the womenfolk. The employers begged him in vain, telling him that they wanted him to have the job because he was the only educated man out of all the employees because he had Standard Two.

"MaXulu, pleeease!" Sithole says reproachfully whenever they discuss this matter, something they do quite often these days thanks to his wife. This topic makes him feel emotional. It is as if they never talk about anything else any more.

"Except," it's MaXulu's defiance, "except when we talk about your ancestors and the sacrifices they selfishly demand from us when they know that we are starving and they can do nothing about it."

"MaXulu, pleeeease!" The anger in Sithole is brewing. It's one thing to say he should go to look for work at the farm, but it is absolutely something else when someone, whoever she is, talks like that about his ancestors. "MaXulu. Please. Don't start again. If you as much as say another word about this …" What will happen is too much even for his mouth to pronounce.

MaXulu obeys. But the anger inside her is unbearable. This is their only chance to get something and Sithole refuses to take it? Just because he believes some evil spirits will give him a better job? Shit! Why did she marry such a hopeless man?

As the conflicting thoughts run through her mind, Sithole is watching her mouth while it moves about without articulating any sound. She is darker now, a sign that she is really upset. Sithole is touched by his wife's state and wants to console her. Only he does not know how. He was brought up to be a strong Zulu man. Being passionate and caring is a weakness, according to his standards. And it is weak men whose wives haul them by their noses, weak men who care about the feelings of their wives. But now things are bad and even he wants to be kind to his wife.

"Please, my wife, don't be stubborn." He is doing his best. "I always tell you that the ancestors expect us to give, and in return they will give us even more." He looks at his wife, not knowing if the words fulfil his purpose or not. But soon his old self takes over, "I wonder how you even reached Standard Five with that stone-head of yours. A relationship with the ancestors is a give and take. We give and they take, and they give and we take. Just listen to the sound of that! I should have been a poet." He laughs heartily and looks for at least a smile on his wife's face. He only sees anger and disbelief.

Then his wife says, "But we have done nothing but give. Every time we slaughter goats and cattle in this house … We keep on giving but when it is time to take, we have to give more."

"Hmn!" Sithole starts, feeling pity for his wife. "It is clear that you know nothing about these things, MaXulu. But what can one expect from someone who grew up as a Watch Tower, saying our ancestors are demons."

"To tell the truth," MaXulu forgets herself and talks back, "I never actually believed that they are demons. But I'm beginning to now."

"You see?" Sithole almost jumps. "How can we ever have anything if you talk like that about my ancestors? Hhe? Don't you know that they hear us?" Sithole is shouting now. His wife's crazy talk may cause him to slaughter a goat, begging for forgiveness.

MaXulu has her own feelings on this, "No. No. No. Sithole! This is just not working."

Sithole feels like there is a deep void inside him. "As I am telling you, things will be better now. Remember that we have been slaughtering these goats and cattle in a vacuum because my great-grandfather's brother (may his soul burn in hell) turned our ancestors against us by stirring the wrong concoctions."

"You know what?" – it's still the new MaXulu – "I hate hearing that. I just hate it."

Sithole ignores her and goes on, "But Zwane has rectified all that now. I only need to make the last sacrifice to my great-grandfather with a cow and you will see how rich we will become." Sithole can't help smiling when he gets to the part about being rich. "We will be richer even than Hadebe. We will have not one stairway but many."

"This confuses me," MaXulu begins. "There is always a problem. Someone is stirring up black medicine? Someone needs a cow to be slaughtered for them? No. A car without wheels cannot move!" MaXulu almost spits in disgust.

"MaXulu, please! Don't say my ancestors have no wheels. Take it from me. Zwane has rectified everything. You heard with your own ears our grandfather saying that …"

MaXulu does not let him finish. "No, I did not. All I heard was Zwane pretending to be your grandfather and only a fool did not notice that."

"But, MaXulu …"

"No, Sithole. Don't enter into my mouth when I am speaking the truth for once in our marriage. Do you remember that I asked your grandfather his name and he did not know it? Just because Zwane did not know it?"

"I tell you over and over again that you were not supposed to confront my ancestor like that. You could have died or even been struck dumb. A young wife never talks to the ancestors." Sithole is beginning to feel hot and MaXulu does not care.

"And that is why you had to remind him of his name?"

"Oh! Don't be so difficult, MaXulu. Zwane did a great job rectifying our ancestors. Look now, you can feel that there is no strain on our shoulders. We can walk and breathe freely."

"All I feel is hunger," MaXulu says. "And that walking and breathing freely should not have cost us R2 000. We would not be this hungry if you had not thrown that money away."

Sithole takes a deep breath before responding, "Oh. There you go again. Do you think this money would never have been finished if I did not use it to pay Zwane?"

"Of course not. But I will always complain about it as long as we are hungry."

She sends a furtive glance at her husband and notices that the anger is fuming inside him. The devil in her tells her to ignore his anger and continue. "And now you want to take the little we have and make Mkhipheni's feast." The tears that fill her eyes amaze and disappoint her. She doesn't want to be weak any more. "You are wasteful!"

Sithole forcibly hits the sides of the sofa with both his hands. He did not intend to do this, but as he does they both realise that he is angry, really angry.

"MaXulu, pleeeease!" he shouts now. "Let's forget about this because you are just like a child." He pauses for a while, thinking that it would indeed be better to close this discussion here and now. But the anger inside him has reached its saturation point. "It shows that no *mbeleko* was performed for you when you were a child, not to mention *umhlonyane* and *umemulo*. This means you are not registered in your family. You are just floating."

"I'll rather float than be as wasteful as you are. And what is wrong with me that none of those silly rituals were performed on my behalf? What defects do I have?" MaXulu asks confidently, knowing that she lacks no human quality even though she was not brought up the way her husband expects every sane person to have been.

"What about those big pimples?" Sithole says, his face brightening. It's amazing how revenge sometimes heals the soul. Sithole is even able to entertain a dry smile now. "It's not even pimples. It's *ikhambi*."

"But I'm beautiful in spite of them," MaXulu says triumphantly.

Sithole is glad she responds thus. Just what he needs. "Oh-ho! You are just saying that to please yourself." He tries to prevent himself from laughing. "Do you think I was telling the truth when I said it is our tradition that Sithole men don't kiss women? I only said that because I did not know where to kiss you with those giant pimples on your face."

MaXulu feels like screaming. She knows she has a disease that causes the worst kind of pimples on her face, but her husband has always told her she is beautiful in spite of them. He has even tried to convince her that she is beautiful because of them, something she flatly denies. But now he tells her this!

"So why don't you leave me and marry those without pimples? Hhe?" She starts to sob. "You just want me to feel bad." She blows her nose and then says, "You hate me."

"Suit yourself!" Sithole does not care that his wife is in pain. He stands up to leave. When he is in the kitchen, he mutters, "Yes. No one says my ancestors have no wheels and gets away with it."

7

Many people grab their things when the truck arrives. There is too much chaos and no consideration is made for Priest or anyone, for that matter, who is believed to be above others. As the prospective workers chase after the truck, some fall and are run over by the others. The truck is quite big, but it cannot accommodate all these people. Priest sees himself running and struggling with the rest. He tries to turn deaf ears to the kind of language being exchanged:

"Hey, you fool! Why do you tread on me like this?"

"Can't you see that I also want a job? Arsehole!"

But one woman, who is safely on the truck, remembers the importance of the Priest in times like this. "The Priest. Somebody make space for the Priest!"

The truck is now overloaded and many people have given up hope of getting to it. In a moment people try to move themselves, becoming even more compressed. Priest is then told to get into the space that has been made for him. It isn't a space at all but he climbs in, as instructed. All he does now he does absent-mindedly. He is not sure if he is really awake or dreaming.

The way he is crammed on to the truck makes Priest suppose that being on this truck is the most uncomfortable experience he has ever had. He begins to wonder if he is really supposed to be here. If being employed means he has to endure this pain twice every day, it will also mean he will be paying much more for much less. The journey to the farm is about a fifteen-minute drive. All this time Priest sits exactly in one spot, not able to move himself.

It takes about three minutes before Priest is aware of how disagreeably he has seated himself. He learns that he has sat himself between the thighs of a woman who opened them widely, letting him rest his elbows on her knees. He has his legs tightly kept together so that another woman cannot sit between his thighs but rather on top of them. The woman who is seated over him is so close that it is hard for him to pronounce any sound freely. Recognising the situation he is in reminds Priest of his rank in society. He thinks this may be a way of dethroning him. He turns his head to the side and then complains, "Oh God, what have I done to you? Why do you squeeze me like this?"

By uttering this complaint, Priest again attracts a lot of attention to himself. Some feel pity for him and some think they have to laugh.

"Move your legs, you! Can't you see that Priest needs more space?"

"He is used to having too much space to himself in the church. But this is not the church, this is Johnson's truck. We are all equal."

"What do you want me to do? I can't move!"

"But Priest needs space. Tell the others next to you to move and make space for Priest."

Priest hears these voices as if in a dream. He wants to tell the woman who is talking on his behalf to stop, but words do not come out of his mouth. He listens sadly as these people continue to discuss him. He hears the others talk, laugh, swear and sing. He still cannot believe that this is really himself.

It is like a dream come true when the truck finally arrives at the farm and Priest, with his colleagues, alights. Johnson looks at the people and wonders how his truck could have managed such a number of people. He is about forty-eight, tall in height and strongly built. His face does not betray any sense of kindness, and his many deeds confirm this lack.

"What do you think this is?" Johnson bellows at the driver. The driver is frightened when he sees his master becoming red with rage. "Don't you know that I paid money for this truck, or do you think I got it for free as affirmative action?" Johnson alternately points a finger at the driver and the truck as he speaks.

"I tried to control them, Mnumzane," the driver says in a tremulous voice. "They all forced themselves into the truck. I tried to stop them, but they would not listen. They told me that they all want work."

"Do you know how much damage you may have done to my truck? My own money?"

"I know, Mnumzane."

"How much is it?"

"I think it must be a great deal of damage, Mnumzane. I'm very sorry."

"I'm going to check the damage you have caused and I will take it from your salary."

As the above scene unfolds, Priest is watching and listening, wondering at how things haven't changed. When Johnson has finished with his driver, he turns to look at his prospective employees and, as he directs his fierce glance at them, they all look down in fright. Nobody wants their eyes to meet with the grey, cat-like eyes of Johnson.

Johnson brightens up when he realises these people have come because they have nowhere else to go. A few years ago farmers' lives were made miserable by these blacks who now come to them looking for work, suffering and sadness written on their faces and their meagre bodies.

"What have you all come here for?" Johnson shouts after a while, looking at the seekers of employment closely, as if trying to find out if there are any familiar faces amongst them. "What have you all come here for?" he repeats when no one ventures a reply.

Priest, who resides closer to God and the Word, is too much engrossed in his own thoughts to respond to Johnson. So one woman, the one who interrogated Priest about the money and was accused of ugliness, comes closer to Johnson and answers, "We want work. We are hungry."

She speaks with a clear, fearless voice. The others nod their approval. Some even go so far as to articulate words of agreement, saying, "Yes, we want work" or "Yes, we are hungry".

Johnson likes the last word that woman has said. Hunger and destitution force people to accept the most unreasonable terms, especially if they have nowhere else to go. He suddenly remembers a song one of his former employees used to sing when he was drunk: "You will remember me when you've run out of strength." The tune rings in Johnson's mind. These people have really run out of strength, and indeed they have remembered him, the white farmer.

"It's not my fault that you are hungry. Don't say it as if I have an obligation," Johnson states with so much vehemence that many wish they could withdraw the utterances of approval they made when the ugly woman spoke. It is a shame they can't.

"We heard that you wanted workers and that is why we came. I think that is why you sent your truck also. Here we are then."

Before Johnson has his words ready, there ensues a bitter noise among the people. The cause for the chaos is the manner in which the ugly woman demonstrates disrespect for the white man, the people's only hope.

"Why do you talk to *umlungu* like that? Can't you see that you'll blow it for all of us?"

"I told you she needs to be killed," says a man in green overalls.

"Hey, you dog. Don't talk that nonsense to me," the ugly woman growls and takes two steps in his direction. He takes two steps backwards, only stopping when he notices what he is doing.

"If that was me, I would be red with blood now," one man suggests.

"Me too. I have never been insulted by a woman before."

These words find their way to the ears of the man in green overalls. He realises he has to do something to protect his reputation. Instead he says, "South African law strongly disapproves of women abuse."

The people look at the man in green, astonished.

"I don't want to go to jail. My children will have no one to support them." As he utters the last sentence, the man in green remembers that his children have lived for many years without him actually supporting them. When he recalls this fact, he thinks that the others are thinking the same thing, so he decides to correct himself. "I don't want my children to be sorry that I am in jail."

"Peace, everyone. In the name of Jesus, we have come to seek work," Priest puts as much stress as he can on his words.

Johnson, who has looked at these people, trying to find any familiar face but not doing so, is very shocked when he recognises Priest. How greatly seeking employment changes people's looks! Johnson has never seen Priest without his priestly attire before. The fact that Priest is not only without his honourable clothing, but also wearing large old boots and a very tattered overall, moves Johnson.

As Johnson struggles to make sense of what is in front of him, Priest continues, "In the name of the Lord's only Son, we have come to seek employment. Hunger is killing us and our children." Priest pauses and observes the attention with which Johnson is listening. "We have come to offer ourselves to work for you on the terms that best suit you." Priest stops again, looks at the sun, as if asking if it is okay to say what he is going to say next. "We can even work on Sunday if you want."

Johnson sees that these people are just what they've always been, and he despises them for it. Even so, these people are just what he wants. In the last few months he has been trying to decide on the wage for his workers with difficulty. Now he knows with certainty that these people will accept his first offer. He smiles at the enchanting realisation of how much money he is going to save.

"Yes, I do need people to work," Johnson starts in a friendly tone. "As you know, I want to plant trees, so there is going to be a lot of work."

He observes the people's faces lightening as he speaks. Hope, which has been lost, returns to them. They are indeed going to get employed and be able to do something for their families, no matter how little.

"I know that most of you are unfamiliar with the business of planting trees. And those who know it do not know it from a planter's point of view." He pauses and watches the people whose faces have become serious. "So, I'm telling you, it is very expensive. One thing I cannot tolerate is for you to be lazy when I cannot see you."

The people nod approvingly. It's unthinkable that they can be lazy and jeopardise their only hope.

"The only way to avoid that is for you to work on a quota system."

Many people who are familiar with the term look wildly at Johnson. This system is one hundred per cent in favour of the employer. Workers have to work from morning till late without rest.

"I am only prepared to pay you eight cents for every eighty-centimetre hole you will dig," Johnson announces, earning himself a great deal of disapproval from his audience.

The mention of eight cents eradicates all traces of fear from the people. The need for respect is put on the backburner. What does this man think they are? The things one can do with eight cents are absolutely nil. Eight cents have to be more than ten times multiplied before they make a rand, which is now nothing in itself.

"He is mad!" one man protests.

"What can you possibly do with eight cents?"

"This is an insult. This *umlungu* is insulting us."

"We may be hungry, but we are not mad."

Johnson sees that his offer is totally unacceptable to the people. He has anticipated this, so he calls on his second strategy: "If that is not okay with you, I will increase it dramatically by offering you R16." Many people brighten up. It makes them feel content to hear the money translated into rand. But that satisfaction diminishes when they hear how much they have to do to earn the money: "But you will have to dig two hundred holes per person."

Again, this piece of information creates another clash. Does this man think they are donkeys or what?

Priest, who is very talented with numbers, concentrates on counting precisely how much Johnson has added to his previous offer. "It's exactly the same," he shouts, not particularly addressing Johnson or the people. "R16 for two hundred holes is exactly eight cents per hole if you divide." Priest is sad, he is losing his mind, "Oh God, why are you so far away when we need you?"

There ensues a hot debate as to whether the people have to accept Johnson's offer or not. Some see the offer as an insult to their man- and womanhood. R16 is a small amount, but having to dig two hundred holes for it is unthinkable.

"I'll rather die of hunger than be a slave."

"He should take us back to where he took us from."

"It's better not to work than not to work when you are working."

"There is no such thing as an ancestor."

After a great disagreement, those who have done this kind of work before testify that it is humanly possible to dig two hundred holes in one day, although it is very daunting. The worker has to be on the fields by six and work all the way through to six in the evening – six to six, as they call it – with only thirty minutes for rest and eating. When they recall the miserable conditions in which they left their homes, many decide to give it a try. Half a loaf, or even a quarter of it, is better than nothing, no matter how hard you work for it.

Priest has vested so much hope in this job that it is hard for him to refuse it. But what actually motivates him is the thought of his wife back home. If he turns it down, the matter will come up every time there is a problem.

Priest sees by the look on MaDuma's face that she is not happy to see him coming back home so early in the morning. The news has spread all over Ndlalidlindoda that there were so many people who had gone to Johnson's that he was unlikely to need them all. Now, as she sees him, MaDuma thinks her husband has failed to secure himself a job at the farm. She has begun to imagine life if her husband is earning at least something. His failure to get a job affects her badly.

"Johnson is exploiting us," Priest starts as he puts his lunch box on the kitchen table. "He wants us to dig two hundred holes for R16."

MaDuma's disappointment turns to anger. This anger is not directed at anyone in particular but to life itself. But now that Priest tells her about the conditions under which they have to work, MaDuma thinks he has returned because he does not want to dig two hundred holes for R16. She is a sufferer from high blood pressure, referred to as "high-high". When she is displeased, she feels hot and sweats.

"In times like these!" MaDuma starts, breathing heavily, "In times like these, a real man would dig three hundred holes for R10."

When Priest notices his wife's deteriorating temper, he thanks himself for having put his name on the list. He is aware of what his wife is thinking. If he does not clarify the matter soon, the situation could be worse.

"We are going to start work tomorrow. Exactly at seven, we will start digging," Priest tells his wife, and watches as her face changes for the better and her breathing speed returns to normal.

She pronounces a long "Huuuu" and turns her head sideways, thus betraying her happiness at receiving the news. "I knew you would do the right thing," she says with a smile. "You are a real man!"

When Priest and his fellow workers go to work the following day, they sit more freely on the truck since many people have decided to starve rather than be slaves for Johnson. The work is very hard in the fields. They work from seven to five without getting enough rest. Most people, including Priest, fail to dig two hundred holes. Only four people manage to dig the required number. Johnson does not complain. He also does not commend those who succeed. He only urges his induna to record the number of holes each person has dug.

Priest finds the work they have to do very hard. He sees their situation as nothing but slavery. He respects those who have decided against taking Johnson's work. He hates his wife for forcing him to do this farm work. But it is not really his wife. He knows how she was when he was still working at the bacon factory and earning a good salary there. She was kind to him. Then he lost his job and they started to suffer. His family did not know hunger when he was working at the bacon factory. They did not know there would come a time when they would hanker for meat. Now all that has gone and hunger has taken over.

Yes. It is hunger that has forced him into this slavery. Not his wife. If they did not have to do without food, he would not be working here. His wife would not have forced him to go. It is the hunger that has made her think the unthinkable and be so demanding.

On the first day of work Priest does not eat his supper. When he has had his bath, he throws himself on the bed, hoping to rest. The next thing he hears is the voice of his wife telling him it is time for him to wake up and go to work. Priest drags himself to the bath and leaves his home for another day of hard work with his muscles still stiff from yesterday's work.

Yet he works as if he feels nothing. He has given himself to it. If he has to be a slave for Johnson in order to survive, so be it. But the anger inside him is strong. Why is it that they have to suffer like this while other people live better? Why did they vote only to lose their jobs, to suffer from hunger that forces them into this slavery? He does not want to attribute it to anyone or anything. But he, like everybody in his position, knows that something is wrong.

Priest and many others are as unhappy on their first pay day as they are to be for the next fourteen months in which they work for Johnson. Priest earns R225 for twenty-four days of hard work. Many others earn almost the same. Only a few come close to R384, the amount earned for R16 a day. Priest listens sadly as his fellow workers sing on their way back home. They do not sing because they are contented and happy. Their singing is a way of coming to terms with their situation.

When Priest arrives home on the first pay day, the look on her husband's face tells MaDuma that something is wrong.

"Oh God, he did not pay you," the woman says in a troubled tone.

"He did pay us nothing." Priest is very tired and seems to hate everything around him. "Here!" he gives his money to his wife. "This is what I have been working for all this time."

MaDuma cannot help smiling when she sees the closed, brown envelope given to her. Priest has never before given her all his wages, so she is pleased. She does not look at the writing outside that states the name of the payee and the amount paid, so she is greatly surprised and angry when she counts the money and finds that it is only R225.

"Is this all you got?" she asks in disbelief.

Priest does not want to talk. "I'm tired," he says. "I want to sleep."

"But you haven't got your food yet." MaDuma feels sorry for her husband when she sees how depressed he is. "Let me get your food first," she pleads.

"If it's pap and potatoes, don't bother."

"Ah! Go to sleep then."

8

It's one of those days of fatigue when Priest has been toiling like a slave at Johnson's. Right now he is sitting on the sofa in the living room – watching without seeing his tiny, black-and-white television – while in his mind he is in bed having a quiet, dreamless sleep. The fact that he is still here is proof enough he has no control over his own body any more. He intended to go to bed thirty minutes ago but his bones and muscles did not comply. They seem to be on strike or something.

Thinking of strikes, why is it that he and his fellow slaves of Johnson do not engage in a strike? Or maybe usurp the farm, like the animals did in one of Sandile's novels he has read? What was it called? Animal something. *Animal Kind* perhaps. Or *Animal Pride*. It doesn't really matter what the title of the book is. They might call theirs *Slave's Pride* or something. But that would be like shitting under a tree that gives you shade when the scorching sun threatens to burn you to death. Not a single one of his fellow slaves would even consider that. Didn't they agree to being slaves because they preferred that to watching their children die?

As such a dialogue takes place in Priest's mind, Sandile steals inside the living room and seats himself on the sofa on the right-hand side of his father. Priest can tell from his expression that there is something the boy wants to say. Usually Sandile does not spend time in the living room with his family. He normally stays alone in his room, reading his books. Priest is too tired to say anything, leaving the boy to decide on his own whether to speak or not. After four minutes, Sandile seems to have garnered the required vocabulary and confidence for him to speak. "I regret to inform you, Father, that blood will be spilled in this place of ours."

Priest hears this as if in a dream or at a distance, and when he has managed to make sense of the disconnected sounds, he suddenly recovers from his half-sleep and the fatigue goes away. He threatens to stand up as he says, "Hhe?" Priest hopes he did not hear his son correctly.

"I say blood is going to be spilled in this area."

"You are mad," Priest says with a strange suddenness and then asks, "Why would you think that?" Priest's body has forgotten about the strike and the tiredness of toiling on the farm. He is now rejuvenated.

"Because I know, Father." As they continue talking, Sandile is getting more and more confident. The fear of talking to his father diminishes as he speaks.

Priest may have recovered from fatigue, but he has no time for nonsense. "You are young and senseless, what do you know?"

"Did you hear about the woman who materialised at Hlanzeni?" Sandile answers his father's question with another.

"What woman? Materialised?" Priest asks in utter confusion.

"See? You don't know everything yourself. Some things pass you by even though you are old," Sandile says in jest, but Priest is annoyed. This is not a proper way for a son to talk to his father. Not if that father is a priest.

"When last did you read your Bible, Sandile? Hhe?" Priest shouts.

Sandile stammers before answering. "It's ... it's been a ... a while, Father." Now he gets his strength back. "But I thought we are not talking about the Bible. We are talking about the blood that is going to flow in this land. We are talking about the pain and the tears, Father. Not some old book without meaning."

Priest sends an annoyed glance at him, his teeth clenched. His eyes have become red. What is this boy saying about the Word of God? His God? Who is this boy in the first place? Isn't he nothing but a dog who depends on him for everything? Priest contemplates punishment and suddenly changes his mind. No use punishing him now. He has not been aware that this boy is growing up and developing his own mind – a mind that is not only influenced by the good tidings of the Lord and the Holy Ghost. The evil forces of Lucifer also influence him. To Priest, things are always divided in two. Life for him is either black or white, good or evil and sacred or profane. His son seems ready to leave the good that is his home for the evil represented by the secular world outside.

Having decided against corporal punishment, Priest orders his son to reconnect himself with the Word of God. He can't give him up to the forces of evil without a fight. "Go and read Exodus 20, verses one to seventeen. Read it aloud three times," Priest roars like a wounded lion. His voice is vibrating with anger, and Sandile need not be told that he will brook no contradiction. "I will be listening and counting."

"But, Father, I know those verses by heart. You used to make me sing them," Sandile complains.

"Certainly you have forgotten them. It's been a while since you last recited them. So do as I tell you!"

Instead of contradicting his father again, Sandile stands up and starts reciting the verses like he did when he was younger: "God spoke and these were his words." Somehow his voice trembles in fear. This act reminds him of his days in junior primary where they were made to recite verses and were punished if they got them wrong. This is what his father did to him too. "I am your God who brought you out of Egypt, out of the land of slavery."

As Sandile utters these verses, Priest's mind is taken back to his thoughts about his own slavery and that of his fellow workers. God really has liberated them from the slavery of apartheid and white domination and oppression. But something has gone wrong along the way. Perhaps Moses and his brother Aaron decided to join forces with the Canaanites and the Philistines. It is amazing that the Bible was written so long ago and so far away but it speaks directly to them. Priest and other poor people of Ndlalidlindoda are the Israelites on their way from Egypt.

Priest's mind comes back when his son recites, "You shall not make wrong use of the name of the Lord your God; the Lord will not leave unpunished the man who misuses His name …"

"Hear that?" Priest intervenes gladly. It is as if God has suddenly appeared to support him. "The Lord will not leave unpunished the man who misuses his name. You should get that into your head."

Fatigue has completely vanished from Priest's system. His son's blasphemous talk has really boosted his energy. But now, as he continues talking, his voice is calmer, "It is a bad thing, son, to talk badly about the Bible, as if you are talking about your friend. The Bible is God's own words. It is the manifestation of God's words and if you defy it, you defy God Himself and you will not win. You can never win."

As he talks now, there is no longer anger in his voice. Perhaps the fact that his son has kept the good words inside him all this time is what pacifies him. This calls forth the book of Deuteronomy to his mind: "These commandments which I give you this day are to be kept in your heart; you shall repeat them to your sons, and speak them indoors and out of doors. When you lie down and when you rise." Yes. This is exactly what he has done. He is glad his son has kept the good words in his heart. But does he understand and believe them? Well, that is another question. God will have to see to what happens inside his son's head. He cannot.

"Except …" Sandile says after a while, making sense of his father's words.

"Except what?"

"Except, if I am as powerful and cunning as Jacob, I may be able to beat God."

The anger in Priest returns tenfold. He looks at his son with trepidation, wondering if Satan has not taken over his son's thinking. All the words he knows seem unable to convey what is inside him, so he decides to remain quiet.

It is his son who speaks again after a while. "Do you entirely believe in the Bible, Father?"

That Priest can answer, even in deep sleep. "Yes. Body and soul." Saying the words provides him with a tinge of happiness. Lucifer may have got his son, but he certainly hasn't got him.

"So you will agree with me," Sandile continues. "You will agree with me that if God were visible and in human form it would be possible for a strong person to beat him?" Sandile cannot help smiling.

His father darkens with rage. "Would you tell me what kinds of books you have been reading lately? Because you seem to me to be heading straight to the dark side with those heretic thoughts and questions." Priest feels hot now. Being in the same room with Lucifer is no easy matter. Sandile seems to be blind to his father's anger. Or doesn't he care?

"No, Father. I haven't turned to the dark side. As for the books I read, the Bible is still the first among them." He pauses again, lest he begins to laugh. He then continues, "I am pleased to tell you that I enjoy its poeticality. Whoever wrote it is a genius. They had great knowledge of literature at its best."

"Oh God, what have I done?"

"But why do you lament like that, Father? Don't you know that the character who is Jacob in the Bible fought with the other who is God and won?" Another laugh disturbs him. "Well, he did not actually win. It was some kind of a draw," Sandile says, and watches in wonder the transformation in his father.

Priest's face looks as if he is going to explode. "You know what?" he says, when his breathing has slowed. "Let's stop this conversation because you certainly are someone I do not know." His voice is full of sadness as he stands up, getting ready to leave. "If you want to go to Gehena you are free to do so, but please don't take me with you. I do my best to be able to get to heaven when my time is over. So, as they say, 'Stay away from me, Lucifer!'" He rushes out of the living room. Mentioning Satan's name makes Priest believe that he may indeed be with them.

Sandile laughs when his father has disappeared down the passage. I wonder why people like Father claim the Bible is God's Word but when you mention some verses they act as if you have become a follower of Satan, he thinks.

After a while Sandile leaves the living room. He goes to his bedroom, but this is no time for him to sleep. Instead, he decides to read his poetry. Reading his own work completes him somehow. He may not be published, but that doesn't matter. He will always write, because for him the act of writing and reading what he has written is therapeutic. He often wonders how people who do not write fiction manage to deal with the complexities of life and their suffering.

Although today I'm like this;
Clad but in tattered sacks
My butt's laughing behind my back
Torches telling everyone I'm a hobo.
Don't look down upon me.
I was not born like this.

Although now I am like this
Have no education, no civilisation
The languages of power
I do not speak.
Do not laugh at me.
I too am of blood.

The fact that he is the one who wrote what he is reading makes it even more of a diverting read. Even hunger shies away if he is reading his work. Perhaps one day he will be published, but for now his writings are for his own amusement and healing.

It is ten minutes to eleven when he finally retreats to his bed. The worries of the day are now out of his system. He can have a nice, peaceful sleep. But before he falls asleep, his father's knock disturbs him. "Sandile! Wake up! Open the door."

Sandile can tell by the sound of his voice that his father has been in a deep sleep. Whatever has woken him up? An unpleasant dream perhaps? But his father has never come to him for comfort before. He hurries and opens the door for his father, whose eyes are reddened by sleep.

"Tell me about the blood," Priest says, still groping to find Sandile's bed. The words come as a great surprise to the boy.

"Father, are you sure you have woken up?"

"Yes, Sandile," Priest answers. "I'm here in your room. Just tell me about the blood you said is going to be spilled in the area." Priest is now seated on his son's single bed.

"I don't think it's a good idea, Father …"

"Just tell me!" Priest snaps, and Sandile realises that this man who is half asleep means business.

"I don't know where to start," he begins, and then stops again, his mouth showing that he is trying. "Is it okay if I start by asking about the woman of Hlanzeni? Have you heard anything about her?"

"No," Priest says proudly, "I know nothing about her and I want you to tell me everything you know. Everything."

"They say that last week Sunday the people at Hlanzeni woke up to find there was a new house where there had been none the previous day." He stops and steals a furtive glance at his father. Priest's mouth is agape with wonder and intrigue. "It is said that the chief then sent a delegation of men to find out what was going on. When they got there, the men found an old woman who was busy sweeping the floor. She was doing nothing except sweeping the floor and it looked to those men as if that was all she did. Isn't that strange, Father?"

"Not as strange as the house suddenly appearing where there has been none the previous day," Priest claps his hands. "But it is strange indeed."

"The men asked her who she was and where she came from. She told them she was sent from above to 'sweep away' the youth because they have lost the way. Or, should I say, we have lost the way? She said the youth no longer have respect for God and the elders and therefore they have been condemned to death. She was sent to sweep them off the face of the earth."

Sandile pauses and Priest says, "How does the blood come in? I'm more interested in what you said about the blood. Just tell me about blood!"

"Hmn," Sandile feels tired now, "this is a bit complicated, Father, and you came when I was about to fall asleep."

"Just tell me what you were going to tell me." Priest does not budge.

"The thing is that I have just written a short story."

"And?" Priest's impatience is almost visible.

"I wrote a short story that tells a story exactly like the one of the woman I have just told you about. Only it was our neighbours, the people of Canaan, who were swept away. All those who get fat out of the blood of the poor." Sandile pauses and looks at his father. He notices that his eyes seem as though they are going to pop out.

"I still remember that when I wrote that story it was about half past three in the morning. I just woke up and started writing. I do not know where such great inspiration came from but it was like I had to write or else … I just had to write, and I was not sure what I was writing. At times I want to believe that I dreamed the story, but if you dream you have to wake up and remember. I did not remember anything when I wrote. I was sort of possessed."

Priest gazes at his son accusingly and says, "What-about-the-blood?"

Sandile continues as if his father has said nothing. "Now the same thing happened the day before yesterday. I woke up in the middle of the night and wrote a story. I did not know what I was writing until I had finished and read it." There is a sense of sadness in his voice now. "I can feel that the story is a representation of what is really going to happen, Father. The title of the story is 'River of Blood'. I did not name it. It named itself!"

Priest passes a distrusting eye over his son.

Sandile continues, "In the story so much blood is spilled that people end up having to drink it instead of water. All the wells and taps ooze blood. It's blood everywhere. Blood! Blood! Blood!" Sandile sings the last words.

"Shut up!" The image of gulping a glass full of blood his son has managed to conjure up makes Priest want to vomit. "Don't say that! I don't want to hear it!"

"But, Father, I thought you craved blood."

"What?" Priest shouts and stands up, as if wanting to thrust his fist at Sandile. "What did you say?"

"I don't mean like drinking it, Father. I thought you wanted to hear the word."

Sandile looks at his father and pities him. He still doesn't know what brought him to his room, but he can see that something is worrying him.

"I regret I came here in the first place," Priest says grudgingly as he makes to leave. "I shouldn't have come to you. You've made me feel worse."

He bangs the door behind him, leaving Sandile still wondering what he should have done for his father. Maybe he wanted me to ask him if he had had a bad dream and then soothe him? Just like a father does to his son.

9

It is a Monday morning at Bambanani High School and Bongani is alone in his office. His fragile mind is not only troubled by the hangover – which he suffers every Monday anyway – but there is something particular on his mind as he paces up and down in the office. Some inaudible sound issues from his mouth that is rarely completely shut.

At some point in his life Bongani came across an expression that "cleanliness is next to godliness" and made it his personal motto. Now, every day before he starts work, he spends time making sure that his office is one hundred per cent neat. Everything has to be kept in its correct place. But today Bongani has forgotten about the filing and is concentrating on something that has caused him much worry.

Right now on his desk there are two books that he has been reading, or trying to read. One of these, red in colour and therefore symbolising danger and spilled blood in Bongani's eyes, is *Counter Communism*. The other, not opened, is *Progress Through Separate Development: South Africa in Peaceful Transition*. The former text is opened on page eight, proof that Bongani had been reading it in the last few minutes.

But what wrought his mental torture is caught under his armpit. It is a manuscript: a collection of poetry by Sandile Gumede. Initially, he was enthusiastic about honouring the poor boy's creative attempts by taking his precious time to read his simple words. Now, simple as they may be, he wholeheartedly regrets he ever set his eyes on the filthy words. Yet he is also glad because, had he not read the poems, he would not have been aware that Sandile is a menace to society.

And he has the snobbish Ma'am Mchunu to thank for that because she is the one who brought him the poem that Sandile wrote for her granddaughter. Ma'am Mchunu's condescension coaxed her to do all she possibly could to prevent her granddaughter from having a relationship with someone from as hopeless a place as Ndlalidlindoda. One of the things she did was to confront the principal of the boy's school and make him stop the Hunger-Eats-a-Man creature from ever communicating with her granddaughter again as he was ruining her prospects in life. When she visited Bongani at his home – because she maintained it was unhealthy to go to him in Ndlalidlindoda – she even advised Bongani to threaten the boy with expulsion from school if he did not stop his silly advances towards her granddaughter.

But what is considerably more important to Bongani is that he has learnt about Sandile. When he read the poem Ma'am Mchunu brought to him as proof that the good-for-nothing boy has a crush on her granddaughter, Bongani told Sandile to bring all his poems so that he might "peruse" them whenever, and if ever, he got the time. This was before he even spoke to him about his relationship with Ma'am Mchunu's granddaughter. Now he is completely disappointed in the boy. Sandile and his diabolical ideas will cause trouble and he needs to be halted by any means. Hence Bongani has borrowed *Counter Communism* from the library, to take a leaf out of the late government's book. How did they deal with the terrorists? That is what he wants to find out.

"The little vampire is over-expressing himself!" Bongani mutters.

Why on earth does the boy write all this nonsense instead of writing about the beauty of nature? Can't the little weasel take a glance at the sun and find inspiration there? A mere glimpse of the moon and the stars can trigger a creative mind and issue quatrains and sonnets of outstanding beauty and purity. Not this nonsense! Why does he not listen to thunderstorms and the deafening thumping of hailstorms on to the iron roof of his house and then write about that? Or the colourful rainbow after such a storm? But the boy chooses to write unpatriotic nonsense about our government, turning a blind eye to all the good that has been done and accentuating – even exaggerating! – all the little shortcomings of our leaders. What did we do to him? Is he so ignorant as to not even know that the time for this kind of criticism is over?

"But what can one expect from someone who lives in an area that is predominantly IFP?" Bongani asks himself and his anger is half healed. What Sandile's poems are saying may be true, but no patriotic son of the country is supposed to notice that. Is it not true that we have a black government now? Isn't our Premier as black as this asinine weasel? But that is to be expected from someone who belongs to such a party. A party whose shitting days are numbered anyway. And if he is not IFP, why would he write this nonsense? Because what he has written is utter rubbish. Look at this! He looks again at the manuscript and begins to read aloud, trying hard to utter each word with as much rancour as he possibly can:

Where has my sweat gone?
As I was running and struggling,
Singing he will come; he is coming,
Hoping soon dawn will come,
And all darkness vanish,
While no belly grumbles.
But still there is mud
On my plate!

Words like these need not be articulated. No. Had they not been mere words, he is sure that they would stink. In fact, they do even now. This boy is rotten inside and he wants to putrefy other people's brains. But he will do that nonsense somewhere else, not here! Not where Bongani Hadebe is in charge of community development and is working his way to becoming a mayor. No ways! No Nkatha will cause trouble in this area.

"This boy will have to be stopped, one way or another," he mutters, and some evil force pulls his attention to the poem in front of him. Why should he care about this rubbish? But somehow he does care. There is something about the poems that makes him want to read on, despite the mistaken views of the boy. He hurls the whole bundle against the wall, to prevent himself from reading through them again. Pieces of paper scatter all over his office. His breathing accelerates and his nostrils widen. He waddles back to his seat. The red book is still there, opened. But before he picks it up, he contemplates the papers scattered in his office. If only it was Sandile's brains scattered like this! Yes. How much he would like that. Sandile's brains scattered all over his office. No. Not his office, but scattered for sure. The thought of a dead Sandile with his crazy brains open for the whole world to see is a gratifying antithesis to reading the poems. Has the silly boy ever heard of Proudly South African?

Now he returns his attention to the book he has only just started to read. There must be something here to help him. Them. All those who love our country. And peace. He reads aloud from the book because he cannot at all read without pronouncing the words. He gave up on trying to learn that art when he was young. There was a time when he saw this inability as a weakness. But now he has realised that it is in fact a gift. Perhaps he is the only one in the whole world whose nervous system recognises the importance of sound in conjuring meaning. Words can only have meaning if they are allowed to speak, and they speak only through the voice of the reader. Not the reader's heart or mind. Never! As he reads, these words pass before his eyes: General Malan … black nationalism … decolonisation … Soviet-inspired … total onslaught … Marxist.

Bongani shudders as he reads. "Bloody Karl Marx!" he feels like spitting. "What a fool! I wonder why he got so famous with his empty skull. But fame is not only for smart people, even if it should be." The idea of Marxism is most appalling to Bongani. What would be the point of living if there is no competition? If there is no rich and poor? Reading further revives him a bit: South African response … total strategy … political … economic … psychological spheres … military.

Yes. This is exactly what is needed. Total strategy to counter total onslaught. He suddenly stands up. He beats his forehead with the palm of his hand. This is what you do to the public phone if it swallows your coins. He knows that he is familiar with the term "strategy", but somehow it eludes him. The problem with these English words is that they are easy to forget. Sometimes you can feel that you know the word, but when you think about it you realise that you don't. Or you are not sure. "It has to do with a plan," a voice in his head tells him. Maybe it's the phone responding after the beating. He smiles when he thinks this. But if so, why didn't they just say "total plan"? This would have made his life easier. Sis! They should read *Complete Plain Words*.

Since he can't be completely certain, he decides to consult his dictionary. "Better safe than foolish!" he tells his book. "Woordeboek!" he announces. If there is anything he likes about Afrikaans it is that the words sound like music. If only he could speak it!

He removes his thick, blue dictionary from the shelf and, as always, starts by weighing it. This reminds him of his boyhood days when he used to buy live chickens. You choose a chicken by weighing it. Looks can be deceiving. The fact that the book he is holding now is so thick is gratifying to him. It is proof that he is a wise man. Having assured himself that his dictionary has lost no weight, he places it in front of himself. "English–Zulu, Zulu–English," the rhythm in what he is reading triggers a little smile. The anger engendered by reading Sandile's profane poems is replaced by the enchantment of hearing good, uncorrupted words. "*Amasu namaqili okuphamba. Empini,*" he reads. The mention of *empini* (in battle) brings him back to the poems. Yes. He will fight this little brat if it's the last thing he does! No Nkatha moron will sow evil ideas here!

"Good morning, sir," a voice says softly and Bongani almost jumps.

"Oh! It is you, Sandile."

"You wanted to see me, sir?"

"Yes, yes. Of course. I want to speak to you."

Bongani looks at Sandile, whose eyes are fixed on his intellectual property scattered around the principal's office. Bongani does not care that Sandile has seen his work floating everywhere. He cannot be scared of some boy in his own school. His eyes move around, trying to locate a particular poem, which is fortunately not on the floor because he put it aside earlier for discussing with the boy.

"Oh, here," he tells both Sandile and himself when he has located it. "I remember now why I called you." He tries to sound wiser, but the words are, as always, devoid of life. If only he could speak Afrikaans!

Sandile looks at the principal and says nothing.

"See this?" Bongani orders Sandile, handing him a piece of paper. Sandile takes it and reads it absent-mindedly. His attention is still on the papers on the floor.

Bongani speaks, "Now tell me, do you have an idea who may have written these nice words?" He releases a mocking smile. They both know he knows Sandile wrote the poem.

"I wrote it, sir."

"Oh! You wrote it? Who is the lucky lady, if you don't mind my asking?"

"It's the girl I love, sir."

Bongani laughs wildly at this. Is it possible to laugh in a foreign language?

"Wow! The girl you love, hey? Where is she right now?"

"She is at her school, at Grey's High."

"And Grey's High is where?" Bongani tries to sing the question.

"It is in town, sir."

"And where are you?"

Sandile wants to strangle him now. "I'm here."

"Tell me the place," Bongani says portentously. "Where are you?" he shouts.

Sandile takes a moment to consider. He knows, like everybody else, that the principal is far from being smart. But this is too much even for Hadebe. "I'm here in Ndlalidlindoda," he says, as if in pain.

"Yes." Bongani likes this name, but prefers to say it in English, "Hunger-Eatsssss." He glances around the office, as if there are other people besides the two of them. Some people say even the walls can hear. Let those in his office hear him now. "Hunger-Eatsss," he repeats, in case either Sandile or the walls did not hear the first time. "Now don't you think it will make more sense if you found the one you love, as you say, here in Hunger-Eatsss? Where you live? Where you belong? Don't-you-think-so?"

"That is a difficult request, sir. It's impossible," Sandile says without thinking.

"What?" Bongani shouts. "Did I say it was a request? Hhe?"

"I thought you did, sir. But either way, it's impossible."

"Are you challenging me, boy, or what?"

"I'm telling the truth, sir."

"Hey, son! Hey, son!" he points a finger at Sandile and stands up. "You don't know me!"

"I know you, sir," Sandile says calmly. He is unaware that he is being impolite.

"Maybe you do not know that I am not afraid of you. It's not too much for me to wait for you after school to have a fairer fight."

This is really funny and Sandile struggles not to laugh. He touches his mouth and says nothing.

"You are doing all this because we are no longer allowed to cane you." Bongani is overwhelmed by the desire to kick and box. "Why don't we do it after school when no law prohibits me from beating you? Hhe? Man to man, after school?"

"Oh, you mean boy to boy, sir?"

Bongani blackens with rage. "I'm going to kill you, poor Hunger-Eateeeaan!" He says the last word louder than the others.

10

In the area that is the buffer between Hunger-Eats-a-Man and Canaan is built Gxumani Community Hall, and this may be said to be the Rainbow's earnest attempt to bring together the two communities whose racial difference has given way to class difference. Gxumani Community Hall is mainly used by the community of Canaan. They use it for functions like weddings, meetings and beauty contests in which people from Hunger-Eats-a-Man are allowed to participate, although they seldom, if ever, win.

Some lucky people from Hunger-Eats-a-Man got themselves employment in Canaan. These are normally women who work there as domestics, cleaning and washing for their masters and also taking care of their children. Sometimes these lucky women can be seen taking their young masters to school or crèche. Many people from Hunger-Eats-a-Man tried but failed to get employment in Canaan. In fact, it is hard to find employment anywhere.

MaDuma seldom goes to Canaan because she does not work there, and she does not or cannot have any friends there. Yet she sees a lot of it from her home or when she is going to town via Canaan. MaDuma has a relative there, her cousin Victor, but his wife made it clear from the start that she does not want to have anything to do with people from Ndlalidlindoda or any relative of Victor's for that matter, because she only married him and not his family.

MaDuma has only once entertained the possibility of seeking work in Canaan but soon decided against it, realising that she cannot manage to work for a black person like herself, especially not for another black woman. She believes that black people, especially black women, oppress other black women if they have the privilege of being their employers. But it hurts her to see the women who work in Canaan come with their groceries when they have been paid their wages, which, as the employers in Canaan have agreed, will never be more than R800 a month. Although she does not like this amount, she envies those who come handling plastic bags from Spar and Shoprite and longs for the smell that these plastics have. However, when that longing makes her feel sad, she consoles herself, "It will be finished in one week!"

Sometimes she spits forcibly and goes to hide inside; sometimes she forgets to spit and just runs inside.

It is a cloudy Sunday morning as MaDuma leaves her home for Canaan Hall, as the people of Ndlalidlindoda mockingly refer to Gxumani Community Hall. The last time she went there was three months back when she attended a meeting of the Grinding Stone, the Gxumani Women's Organisation, of which Nomsa is the leader. The Grinding Stone was started as the Canaan Women's Organisation, expanding only in 1995 to include the starving community of Ndlalidlindoda. Many women of Ndlalidlindoda were very pleased when they were called upon and encouraged to join their well-to-do and educated fellow women in the Grinding Stone. MaDuma was not interested at first because of the pride and self-centredness of the people of Canaan. But now she has become a dedicated member and has noticed, with a bit of concern, that she is gradually getting fond of Nomsa despite her hatred of anything Canaan.

It is 8.50 a.m. as she arrives at Gxumani Community Hall and the meeting starts at exactly nine o'clock, as scheduled. Nomsa is very strict about punctuality, and many women love and fear her. She has said many times that she wants to put an end to the silly notion that if a meeting is said to begin at nine, it means it will start at ten.

MaDuma fears Nomsa just like the others, although she tries by all means to deny it. When Nomsa is angry and shouting, everyone does not feel well.

"Okay, women!" Nomsa hits the table in front of her as she calls for the attention of those still whispering to one another. "Let's begin!" she says loudly.

MaDuma thinks Nomsa is pleased to hear all the women keeping quiet, as if the angel of death is close at hand. The little bitch is indeed the angel of death! Why is it that even I am frightened by her? Maybe she uses some spells to frighten us. MaDuma remembers a story she heard in the news on the radio about a woman who stole a child and cooked him in order to enhance her position in the church.

Nomsa asks – or rather orders – Ma'am Mchunu to open the meeting with prayer, and MaDuma has a feeling of *déjà vu* when she learns that the woman is from Canaan. Ma'am Mchunu is a retired teacher and her title of "Ma'am Mchunu" has remained with her as some kind of an emeritus title. She taught for about thirty-eight years at Thuthukani Primary, acting as principal in sixteen of those years. All these thoughts run through MaDuma's head as Ma'am Mchunu is praying, balancing herself on a walking stick without which she cannot stand on her own.

"We also pray that you liberate us from male oppression and protect us and our daughters from men who have become animals who rape and kill us."

Many women cry "Hmn", and even MaDuma comes back from her mental wanderings.

"We ask all this in the name of Jesus Christ. Amen!"

"Amen!" the women say in unison.

When Ma'am Mchunu drags her leg to her seat in the first row of chairs, Nomsa goes to the front and again addresses the Grinding Stone. She starts by thanking the women for their presence in what she thinks is the most important meeting they have ever had. "I am saying that because today we are going to discuss what I call 'the bestiality of men." The wording interests some women so much that they feel obliged to ululate and others concur by saying, "They are beasts" or just "Yes".

"But before we begin, I want to read you some of the newspaper clippings I have got with me to show you what I mean when I say these men are nothing but animals."

She takes about twenty minutes reading these excerpts, each of which involves a story of some kind of violence against women. Some of these stories are about rape and others about other kinds of domestic violence. She reads all the stories that are short and summarises the longer ones, underscoring the main points.

"This is about a seventy-year-old man who raped his six-year-old granddaughter." She pauses for a moment, allowing the story to sink into the minds of the women. "Thanks to our efforts against the patriarchal legal system, the bastard is serving a life sentence in jail. It's a pity, though, that this is likely to be the shortest life sentence ever. But we hope that the filthy thing will continue his sentence in hell if he dies soon, as I believe he will."

The women welcome the thought with ululation, and many are convinced that if the old man dies, there is certainly no place for him in heaven.

In another story, a man is accused of raping his two daughters of nine and twelve years respectively. When the little girls testified in court, they stated that their father had been sleeping with them for a long time and had told them this is a normal thing that every father does to his children. He said it is so important that it is never spoken about. The women cannot help groaning at this.

Nomsa cannot hide her anger as she reads this story for the tenth time. "The most disgusting thing is that this beast claims to be a priest!" Nomsa says in a voice filled with anger.

This piece triggers noise among the women as they ask themselves, without hoping to find an answer, "What has happened to the men who once lived in this world?"

When Nomsa mentions the fact that the culprit is a priest, MaDuma almost jumps in fright. It takes about a minute before she is able to assure herself that, if it was her husband Nomsa was talking about, she would have known. But the thought of a priest having done something like that troubles her. If one priest can do it, why can't another one do it as well? She suddenly recalls a day when they heard on the radio the story of a minister who was accused of molesting young boys. Priest said that the devil likes the people who try to serve God because the devil is God's rival. Maybe he was trying to tell her something …

MaDuma is rescued from the troubling thoughts by Nomsa, who shouts for quiet in the room. "Have you also become animals?" she demands harshly. MaDuma is astonished at how the stories affect Nomsa. "Have you also become men?"

The women sing "No", "Not a chance" or " No ways". For a moment, being a man is considered the filthiest thing in the world.

When MaDuma looks again at Nomsa, she notices for the first time that she has a very round face and her cheeks look like a fat cake. This is only visible when Nomsa's anger has reached its highest point.

"How would you feel if it was your husband who did this? Hhe? Don't you see that we should do something to protect ourselves from these men?"

The hands hit the air in agreement, "Yes!"

The enthusiasm with which the women accept the idea of doing something pleases Nomsa.

"If only it was possible to get rid of them all!" one woman laments.

"She who is barren is blessed!" another offers.

Nomsa hears and corrects her, "She who chooses not to have children blesses herself!"

The women acclaim.

When that noise has subsided, Nomsa continues with her reading. She tells the Grinding Stone that she is now reading from the local newspaper, *The Eye of the People*. "This means that the perpetrators of these evil deeds live with us in our community."

Murmurs follow this, but Nomsa continues as if she has heard nothing. "I think those of you who live in Ndlalidlindoda – and we should change that name now that we are free – you know Dlamini, who has been raping his eleven-year-old daughter for only God knows how long." Nomsa pauses for a while and her cheeks become rounder as she adds, "To prove that this is an animal, when he was asked why he did such an evil thing, he said it was his duty as a farmer to taste his fruit first, before selling it in the market!"

Even the quietest of the women utters some words of disbelief at this. The problem is that this man was only arrested for nine months and was released when his docket disappeared from court. The noise resulting from hearing Dlamini's story is stronger than that caused by earlier stories. The impact is made more acute by the fact that it is close at hand. It is impossible to imagine it cannot happen to you if it happened to a person you know.

Before the noise has completely subsided, Nomsa reads another story, which is as bad as the previous one, if not worse: "This is about a young man who was found having sex with his mother!" Nomsa allows the women to utter their anger and disbelief, and then continues, "Hmn! I can't believe this. The woman to whom this was done is a helpless disabled woman!"

The noise that follows is not the horror and disbelief of before. It looks as if the women have come to a resolution and Nomsa demands, "What is going on, women of the struggle? Why is everyone standing up? I am not finished here and I want you to listen!"

MaDuma is at the centre of the voices that are speaking at the same time. She turns toward Nomsa and says, "We think it's no use lamenting these violations without action. Instead of recounting these evil deeds and in the process hurting ourselves even more, we think it's better to pay a visit to these two men you have just spoken about."

This is followed by many shouts of "Yes" and the noise of women beating the tables.

Nomsa is both gratified and frightened by what is happening.

It is good that the women have understood the gravity of their predicament. But taking the law into their own hands is problematic. It involves violence, and violence has bad repercussions. As the leader, she will be held responsible for anything silly the women may do.

"No! Women, don't! Taking the law into our own hands will make things worse!" For the first time, as the leader of the Grinding Stone, Nomsa feels the pain of being negated by the women she is leading.

But the women leave from the back door without caring whether she consents or not. Outside it is MaDuma who has taken on the leadership and Nomsa marvels at how well she sings the slogans.

"Down with animals, down!"

"Down!"

"Down with men, down!"

"Down!"

"Down with dogs, down!"

"Down!"

"Forward with women, forward!"

"Forward!"

"Forward the struggle, forward!"

"Forward!"

11

The Grinding Stone has left the hall toyi-toying and singing. They are joined on the way by more women and men who like action. Before they reach Shiyabazali it is decided that five strong and able-bodied women should run to the Ntshangase home and make sure that Muntukabani is there and does not run away before the whole group arrives. If he is not there the crowd will go to Dlamini's place.

As the women nominate those they trust, a name is suddenly created for the five women as the Special Five. MaDuma leads the Special Five, and in no time they reach the Ntshangase home. It is, according to MaDuma, big but without a plan. It looks as if it was meant to be a hall or crèche, anything but a house.

MaDuma and MaShandu enter the Ntshangase homestead, leaving the other three women outside to check that their prey does not try to outwit them by leaving through the back doors and over the fences. When the two women are on the veranda, they wait and listen, hoping to make out if Muntukabani is inside or not. MaDuma holds the tip of her forefinger to her mouth as she tiptoes closer to the door. She hears the man's voice speaking inside and cocks her ears. She also hears the woman who is mute struggling to communicate with her son, but in vain.

"You see?" It is a man's voice.

MaDuma's ear almost touches the door now.

"I told you that I won't beg you! I told you that if you don't want to give me, she will."

The words and sounds do not tell MaDuma enough, so she decides to go and peep at the window in which one of the six panes is broken. She slowly pushes the curtain aside. It takes a while before she grasps what is going on and, when she does, she closes her mouth with the palm of her right hand.

MaShandu opens her mouth without making any sound and asks what MaDuma has seen. MaDuma waves for MaShandu to come and see for herself. After having seen the whole of Muntukabani and his complaining pet, MaShandu slowly reverses, turns and takes two steps back before she vomits.

Muntukabani hears her and demands harshly who is at his door. "I don't want to be disturbed right now! I am busy. Go away!"

MaShandu continues to vomit and MaDuma calls the three women outside to come quickly since their prey has noticed them. When the others arrive, MaShandu is still stooped and her hand is next to her chin. "What I saw today, I hope I never see again," she says when she has enough air.

"Was he having it with her again?" Zodwa demands curiously.

"There is a dog inside" is all MaDuma can say.

Under the circumstances this sentence proves to be meaningless. To the three women who have seen nothing it means that the dog, Muntukabani, is inside, but the women want confirmation that he was raping his mother again.

MaDuma sees they have misunderstood and again prepares to do her best. Her mind is so affected that she feels as if she owns no vocabulary. "There are three people inside," she says with difficulty, before correcting herself. "There are two people and a dog."

The look on Zodwa's face tells her that she does not understand.

"He had the dog in front of him!" is all that MaDuma can bring herself to say.

At last the three women, starting with Zodwa, begin to grasp the situation.

"I think he needs to be killed!" Zodwa says, heading for the window, hoping to see for herself, but by now Muntukabani has left the dog. She is disappointed but not discouraged, so she goes back to the gate where the Grinding Stone has finally arrived.

"You won't believe what we have seen!" she says loudly, and the women who are in front demand enthusiastically to know what indeed they have seen.

"There is a dog inside there!" she points a finger at the house and is pleased to see some of her audience feeling the same agony that she felt when MaDuma could not tell her.

The others shout, "What?", and Zodwa continues, "There are two people inside, and a dog."

Nomsa finds that she cannot take it any longer so she yells, "Can someone tell us what has been happening here? Is the man we are looking for present?"

MaDuma has composed herself and is beginning to be able to get a grasp on her vocabulary. She still feels, however, that what has happened needs to be expressed in as few words as possible. "We found him having sex with a dog in front of his mother!"

All the women who are close enough to hear articulate their disgust and disbelief in different ways, and the news is transferred from the front to the back as if by some kind of wire.

"Let's kill this filthy thing right now!"

"Today we are going to spill blood!"

"Why did God create men in the first place?"

Nomsa is among the very few who care to use their minds now. The others just want to kill the bastard and get it over with. He does not deserve to live in the same world with them. "Let him go to his home in hell."

"Now listen, women!" Nomsa calls them to order. "We should not think with our hearts even though what is happening around us is so disgusting." The noise subsides a little, but Nomsa can feel that what she is saying has very little, if any, impact on the women. "Is he still inside, MaShandu?" Nomsa asks.

"Yes. He is inside."

"I suggest we get him out and talk to him!" She tries to say this as forcefully as possible, but receives the negation she is trying to avoid.

"Okay then. Let's cut off his testicles but not kill him. Let's remove that which makes him behave exactly like an animal!" Zodwa cries.

This sounds like a better idea to the women who are hankering after blood.

"Yes, let them be removed!"

"He will never do it again!"

"We want to see them!"

MaShandu is assigned the duty of cutting off Muntukabani's balls. She now has her sharp knife, and as she holds it in her hands, she feels some unknown force take over her body. She remembers her late abusive husband and recalls that she had held a knife like this when she, with her two daughters, stabbed him to death. That happened many years ago, but right now, as she is holding the knife in her hands, she hungers again for the blood of a man. She calls forcibly for Muntukabani to come out, and when he doesn't, she breaks open the door and enters. This is not a difficult task since the only locking mechanism is a bent four-inch nail.

MaDuma and Belina are next to MaShundu as she charges to the corner of the room where Muntukabani is standing helplessly with a stick. The three women get to him at the same time and seize him.

"You filthy piece of shit!" Belina says, and hits him on his back with a brick she is carrying.

"Leave me alone!" Muntukabani does not tire of kicking as he is taken outside the gate of his homestead. By now there are more spectators. When he is outside the gates he says something that makes many people laugh, and yet more feel disgusted. "I want to go home to my mother!"

This sounds to MaShandu like saying I want to go and sleep with my mother or I want to have sex with a dog in front of her. She throws him down violently and holds him with her knee. "Take off his trousers,

MaDuma! Faster!" MaShandu's eyes have become frighteningly red. She does her job so sharply and neatly that it is only after she has finished that she thinks about the horror of holding a man's private parts.

Muntukabani listens for the pain but does not feel it. He is beginning to think that maybe they did not cut him when the agony attacks him with so strong a force that the scream he makes is more of a cry. It looks as if the world has suddenly become dimmer and seems to be upside down.

MaShandu is breathing noisily as she watches the blood ooze out of Muntukabani. The other women are shouting as the man writhes in pain.

"Yes! So that all the men will know how we are when we have administered an enema!"

"Well done. MaShandu, you have made him an in-between. He is neither man nor woman now."

"I think MaShandu should keep them because she cut him and did it very well at that. Shaka would have offered her a herd of cattle as a reward for her bravery."

"Yes! Let's reward her with them."

It is about half past two in the afternoon when MaDuma finally arrives home. She has a mixture of feelings she cannot describe and is sure that she has never felt like this before. She tells her husband about the events of the day and he responds that he has already heard. Hearing of someone's testicles being removed frightens Priest so much that he holds his own protectively whenever he thinks about it. But the fact that Muntukabani was having sex with a dog troubles him even more.

"Imagine if she got pregnant," he says fifteen minutes later.

"Who?" MaDuma asks, puzzled.

"The dog."

"She would have to find the father and tell him," MaDuma tries to say it as a joke but there is no humour in her.

12

Bongani has spent the weeks since his beating by Nomsa as a worried man. His wife has shouted at him before and on many occasions she has burnt his things, but she has never before laid her hands on him. He has always known secretly that, if it came to a full confrontation as it did that Wednesday, he was likely to lose because Nomsa is tall and tough. She is also left-handed. As a young schoolgirl she demonstrated her fighting abilities many times. Every time her fighting talents were spoken about, the fact of her left-handedness featured very strongly as an explanation for her rare but useful talent. Bongani, on the other hand, has always known himself to be a coward.

His main concern now is the fact that it has become too difficult, if not impossible, for him to pursue what he sees as the struggle for his manly right. He begins to construct a way forward. This is the best plan that he can come up with under the circumstances.

It is on a Sunday that Bongani informs his wife about a journey he is about to undertake. He tells her that he is visiting his uncle who lives about two hundred kilometres from them in a small town called Manakanaka. He warns her that he may take a long time to return – perhaps the whole day – since he has not visited his uncle in ages, so she should not expect him home early.

At nine in the morning Bongani arrives at Riverside and fills his tank to the brim before he goes to the restaurant for breakfast. He orders an

English breakfast, asking the waiter to include mushrooms and eggs but no bacon. The toast is to be of brown bread and he only wants juice. No tea or coffee. As he eats his delicious food, his mind is far away, in some lonely place he does not know. He thinks of the plan he is carrying out and what it can possibly accomplish. It makes him smile.

Manakanaka is just a long building, and accommodates about seven shops. Across the fence is a railway line, and further down is a display of artwork for sale. Nothing else!

"I wonder what this should be called?" Bongani thinks as he alights from his car. "It certainly isn't a town."

Bongani is glad when he sees people sitting on the bench in the corridor of the single building in Manakanaka. On the door they are facing are the words: "Dr S. Ndlovu". Ndlovu is a popular African doctor in the province. His clients, as well as all those who know him well, call him by his first name, Sgonyela. Next to Sgonyela's consulting room is a room of glass walls. Inside it are two pythons. Bongani feels himself leaning closer to the old woman who is on his left.

A tall man in a white T-shirt and short jeans arrives with what may be a late breakfast for the two fearsome pythons. The man in short jeans drops a live hare and four rats into the glass room. This disturbs Bongani so much that he holds on tightly to the bench as he watches each snake pursue its prey. His attention is taken by the hare, which looks very cute to him, and he identifies with it in an instant.

"Run!" he hears himself say, as he jerks forward in a vain attempt to protect the animal. When the larger of the pythons finally catches it, he struggles to look away. The python is swallowing the hare head first and Bongani cannot help blinking repeatedly as he witnesses the last kicks of the hare.

The door to Sgonyela's office opens and a woman comes out with a man who seems to be her son. As they come out there is a sudden quiet amongst those who are waiting. It puzzles Bongani. Only when the two people have gone out of sight do the discussions start again.

"Do you know if the old man Mdunge has been found or not?" asks a woman with a light complexion and huge breasts. Her face shows that she is a regular drinker of alcohol. Probably the drink that is called *pikiliyeza* (the-pick-is-coming), which is notorious for the fact that it accelerates ageing.

"Yes! He was found dead in the Mpofana River, with his right hand and testicles cut off." The respondent seems not to be a fluent speaker of Zulu. She speaks with difficulty, and now and then she brings in Sotho words.

"I wonder what they do with human body parts," says the woman with large breasts.

"Oh that?" a short, dark, bald-headed man says. "It depends on which part it is. Different parts have different purposes."

Bongani listens enthusiastically as the man, who sounds boastful to him, speaks.

"The head is for the aura," he says with exaggerated emphasis. "If you want people to respect and fear you, the medicine for that is mixed with some pieces of flesh and oils from the head." The bald-headed man feels superior as he folds his arms, having finished the display of his undefeatable knowledge.

"And the testicles?"

Everyone in the corridor is interested in the topic. There are no other conversations.

"Hmn! That's another question, Mother, but I will answer you because you have asked," the bald man says knowingly. He takes a slow, heavy breath before he resumes his speech. "Testicles are used for men who are impotent and those who can't have children."

This affects Bongani so much that he suddenly stands up to leave, but then changes his mind again. It troubles him to hear this because he has come to get some herbs that will make him impregnate Nomsa despite her contraceptive pills. Now, as he hears what the bald-headed man is saying, he is very disturbed. It makes a lot of sense and this worries him. If he leaves? No chances of ever having children. But the thought of using the potions of an *inyanga* after what the bald-headed man has said is very painful.

The door opens again and two men and a woman come out carrying a very sick woman on a blanket. As they pass down the corridor the people on the bench keep quiet and watch sympathetically.

It is when they have disappeared that the bald-headed man speaks, "Hmn! That girl will never recover. They are wasting their time. She is already dead." He has meant this as a joke and is disappointed when everybody either ignores him or looks at him dryly. He is, however, not discouraged. "Did you see her eyes? They were so sunken and white! As if she was meant to see more than we do."

"All this is the work of the whites." The woman who says this is seated near a girl who is also very ill. As they speak, the girl is leaning against the wall and is breathing with difficulty. She is not asleep, but Bongani thinks that she does not hear what is said.

"Why do all these sicknesses affect only blacks and not the whites? No! The whites are the cause of our suffering," continues the woman.

"Yes!" the bald-headed man starts. "They always know if there is a disease coming and they even have names for those diseases before they arrive."

When Bongani finally enters Sgonyela's room, he takes some time contemplating the place, hoping to locate some misplaced testicles, which would make him leave right away. But the room is cleaner than he had expected and Sgonyela, although one of the ugliest men in the world, shows himself to be a man of order. There is a table and a chair where Sgonyela sits and, just next to him on the right, a cupboard with medicines. More medicine is packed in sealed bottles arranged in rows on the shelves on the wall. On top of the table, in front of Sgonyela, are bones, which he uses to foretell for his clients.

After the two men have exchanged greetings, Sgonyela asks Bongani what he can do for him. Only now does Bongani recognise the fact that he should have spent some time preparing an answer to this question. He tries to organise his words and finds that it is not easy. How can he tell this man that he has come to ask for the herbs that will cause his wife, who takes contraceptive pills, to conceive?

He makes inaudible sounds as a way of alerting Sgonyela that he is formulating a reply, when a phrase – "complete plain words" – runs through his head and, without thinking further, he ejaculates, "I want children!"

He sees by an amused look on Sgonyela's face that he sounds ridiculous. When Bongani makes no attempt to elaborate, Sgonyela tells him he hears him and assures him that he has come to the right person because there is no problem in this world that he, Sgonyela, cannot solve. "The difficulty, though, Hadebe, is that you did not bring your wife along. My spirit, and it is always right, tells me that it is your wife who has a problem, but it is 'a young boy' to me."

"No, Father Sgonyela," Bongani replies, "my wife will not agree to use your medicines because she is a devout Christian. She is born-again."

"Oh! So she despises traditional African medicine?" Sgonyela smiles as he speaks and Bongani notices that, at least, he has white teeth. The whiteness of his teeth is enhanced by his black skin. The fact that he has such large pimples makes Bongani sympathise with his teeth, thinking that they should have belonged to a better person.

"No," Bongani answers proudly. "She believes in one God, and His Son."

For a moment Sgonyela keeps quiet. He looks at Bongani and Bongani looks back at him.

"Now because your wife does not believe in African medicine, you cannot make her use it?" Sgonyela asks sarcastically and does not give Bongani a chance to respond. "If her Jesus is so important, why doesn't He give her children? Why doesn't He impregnate her?"

"It's hard to force a person to do something she doesn't want to do," Bongani says in a worried tone. Sgonyela does not know that, if it were possible, he would already have forced her to have children with him. "The truth, Father Sgonyela, is that my wife does not want to have children. She takes contraceptive pills. I was hoping you would give me something to make me impregnate her despite her taking those pills."

Sgonyela suddenly changes colour, becoming darker. "I feel like forcing you out of my place! What kind of a man are you? Hhe? Don't you know that you bring bad luck if you talk such shame to my ears?"

"I did not come here to provoke you, Father Sgonyela, but—"

"Don't call me your father," Sgonyela protests. "If I was your father I would not let your wife piss on your head like this. You are a disgrace to the male population!"

What strikes Bongani is that, as Sgonyela becomes angrier, his voice gets softer. Suddenly Bongani notices in Sgonyela a look of serious meditation. He wishes he could see what is going on in that huge head full of scars and pimples.

"Okay!" Sgonyela speaks at last. "I will help you if you still need my help."

Bongani is afraid to speak, so he just nods.

"I will give you very strong potions to make your wife conceive, despite her taking those pills of hers."

This makes Bongani feel better and he decides to encourage Sgonyela: "You are the only one who can help me have children and God knows I want them so much!"

"Leave God out of it!" Sgonyela reproaches.

"I want you to save my children!" Bongani sounds as if he is about to cry. "Nomsa has denied them life for so long and I would give anything to have them live!"

"Don't worry," Sgonyela consoles him, "you have come to the ultimate doctor. I will make you so strong a man that no pills will prevent you from making babies. You will never again release your manhood in vain."

"Thank you, Father … I mean, thank you, great doctor," Bongani feels happy now. "I want to be a bull. I want to bellow like a bull and each time I do Nomsa should be pregnant. I want to have ten children, Father Sgonyela … I mean doctor."

Sgonyela smiles as he listens to this young man who looks rich and silly.

"I want to be a bull among bulls! I want to be a man!" Saying this to Sgonyela makes Bongani feel as if he is talking face to face with the Almighty.

"You speak as if you already know that the potions I am going to give you require you to eat large quantities of bulls' testicles."

"Yes!" Bongani agrees, confused by the excitement of becoming a father. "I will eat as many bulls' testicles as you want me to. Even more!"

"Good! We can begin to celebrate because it's as if you already have the children. You should think about their names and their futures."

Sgonyela stands up to prepare his medicines now. He mixes and remixes the potions, now and then sniffing at them, and sometimes growling like a lion, which frightens Bongani.

"This is no longer between you and your wife! It's between me and the doctors who make those pills that your wife uses. There is only one way for me to win …" Sgonyela pauses and looks at Bongani, "and that's if you get children." He laughs happily and Bongani is forced to follow suit.

"Isn't it the whites who came with the idea that women should rule over us?" Sgonyela asks.

The situation he is in has confused Bongani so much that he answers without giving the question thought. But his answer does not surprise him. It is the emotions that accompany it that amaze him: "Yes, it's them! They caused all this. Now I have no children." His voice is trembling and it sounds as if the tears are just behind the eyes.

"I will make sure all that changes. Your wife will give you so many children she won't believe it."

Bongani watches as Sgonyela assembles his medicines and puts them in a plastic bag. For a moment he thinks about what the bald-headed man has said and again reminds himself that it is not Sgonyela who cuts off men's testicles and makes others eat them. Besides, he has to think about his children.

Sgonyela then gives him the rules to keep while using his medicines: "Rule number one! Do not eat pork when you use my medicines because it will spoil them." Sgonyela looks at Bongani to see the impact of his words.

Bongani smiles before answering, "That will not be a problem because I do not eat pork at all." Bongani feels pleased as he speaks. His self-esteem is greatly enhanced. "I stopped eating pork when I saw that it burns like a lamp in the dark. It surely is cursed meat."

"Good! You also must not cross the hearth when you are still using my medicines."

"Fortunately, I don't have a hearth in my house. We use electricity," Bongani says triumphantly and Sgonyela laughs.

"I don't mean that. I mean that you must not visit your wife when you are using my medicines."

"I don't understand," Bongani says, and his voice shows that he is disappointed.

"You cannot sleep with your wife when you are still using my medicines."

This surprises Bongani so much that he demands without thinking, "May I ask why?"

"Certainly," Sgonyela says suddenly, as if he anticipated or hoped for this question. "What is the point of charging a battery if you are using it at the same time? Besides, in your case, we want the battery to be extra full."

As unusual as this sounds, Bongani thinks he understands Sgonyela. "I will do as you would like me to do," he says in a voice that lacks the confidence he has shown earlier.

Sgonyela pretends to be in deep thought for about three minutes and Bongani decides it would be unwise to disturb him. When he has come to, Sgonyela introduces the topic of payment.

"I have just been talking to my ancestors about their cow. They want half of it or more right now because yours is a tricky business."

"How much is it going to be?" Bongani does not sound at all concerned, and Sgonyela notices that and relishes it.

"The charms and herbs I am giving you are expensive and hard to find. Most of what I have mixed here come from Kenya and Mozambique, and some from very secret and dangerous sources." Sgonyela looks for a frown on Bongani's face and finds none. "All in all, my payment is five thousand."

"What?" Bongani almost jumps. This is far more than he'd expected. "No, Father Sgonyela, you are killing me," he says in disbelief.

"Why do you complain? What is R5 000 for having many cute young boys and girls who look like their mother?"

Bongani is only able to pay two thousand at the moment. He says he will bring the rest in a few days. Sgonyela agrees and tells him that, if possible, he should bring all the remaining money so that his kings will be pleased with him and they will give him children sooner. Bongani says he will try, and then begins to thank Sgonyela for his willingness to help him.

Sgonyela almost screams, "No! Don't say that! Don't thank my herbs and don't thank me! Just leave and never say goodbye."

Bongani stands up to leave. Never say goodbye?

13

Coming from work, Priest notices a commotion in the Phanekeni section of Hunger-Eats-a-Man where he lives. He sees people running and thinks that maybe the Grinding Stone is attacking another man. It is only when he is at the gate of his homestead that he hears what is going on. Sagilasomthakathi (Witchdoctor's-knobkierrie) has sent a tractor full of potatoes to give to the community.

Sagila is a kind white man who is loved and respected by the people. He obtains his employees from Ndlalidlindoda and transports them in his van every day. In addition to their wages, he offers them potatoes, beans and maize meal every month-end. Sagila is a devout Christian and he tries by every means to impart his belief to his workers and the people of Gxumani, especially those of Ndlalidlindoda, because they are his nearest neighbours, although they cannot hear him if he screams. He has hired a priest and, every day before work commences, they start with prayer. Sagila knows many blacks still believe in the ancestors and do not know that theirs is a false belief. The only correct religion in his view is that of the Saviour God and God's only Son.

Sagila does not want to preach and not practise. Didn't Jesus say that a man needs to love his neighbour as much as he loves himself? So, Sagilasomthakathi now and then sends a tractor full of half-rotten potatoes to give to the starving community of Hunger-Eats-a-Man for free. His workers dump the potatoes wherever they please and the people scramble for them. Sometimes the scramble ends in fights.

Priest watches people running after the tractor, carrying empty sacks and buckets in which to put their potatoes. It looks to Priest as though the whole populace has gone mad. The noise! The excitement! Only for rotten potatoes? God, something is wrong. There are women running with children as if they themselves have become young again. "*Hhayi bo!*" one woman calls to him. "Where is MaDuma? Where is MaMbona? Tell them let's go to collect the potatoes."

"She must have already gone," Priest hears himself respond to the fat woman who is shouting. It is as if she is blowing a war horn. Priest looks at her and sees that she might weigh more than one hundred and twenty kilograms. Yet she manages to run. As she carries her body past Priest's home, he marvels at how some people grow so big out of eating pap toasted in fat.

The woman is known as Thithi, because, despite her age, she is not married. She says to Priest, "Tell Nozipho's mother there to come faster. They will finish the potatoes before we arrive."

"But she's got a young baby and nobody to look after the child for her," Priest complains. Just then he sees his young, short neighbour coming with an empty sack. She goes through Priest's homestead and runs in the direction of the tractor, without recognising or even seeing Priest, who is still looking around in amazement.

"Run, MakaNozipho!" Thithi says. "Look at those people! I nearly left you because you have a young child." Her breasts are moving up and down as she runs down to the big gum tree near to which the potatoes are about to be dumped.

"Ohho! I just threw him on the bed and left," MakaNozipho responds, running after Thithi. "Potatoes are like meat these days."

When all the people who have run to the tractor are gone, Priest stands alone in front of his house. He feels a sudden sadness when he again thinks about what he has seen. These people are really suffering and this has made them behave like animals. But what really worries him is his involvement in all the madness around him. He too felt a tinge of happiness when he found out there are potatoes to be fetched and his wife has gone to fetch them. Feeling happy about the potatoes hurts Priest very much, but he also cannot help his disappointment when he sees many people returning from their journey empty-handed.

"Why are you coming back?" a voice asks loudly. Priest listens attentively for the answer because that is his question as well.

"Those silly farm boys did not dump the potatoes near Cleopas like they said they would do," Thithi responds. She is angry and disappointed, but she still manages to laugh as she speaks. "They went all the way to Mswane. Even if we followed, we would get nothing as many people from Mswane and Eqeleni are running to meet the tractor as well."

One woman, whom Priest recognises as the sangoma, comes laughing all the way. She keeps laughing at herself for the way she has run and pestered her children to run faster, lest they lose the tractor. She lives in Manhlanzini, which is quite a distance from here. She has run for two kilometres after the tractor, and now she comes back laughing, with an empty sack in her hands.

"I told my children to run faster," she repeats for the third time when she is near the gate of Priest's home. Only now does it occur to Priest that the woman is not talking to anyone in particular. "My children said we have lost it." Another laugh interrupts her. "I said, 'Go on. Turn to your right and go all the way to Shiburi.'" She keeps walking and Priest hears her still laughing when he can no longer see her.

MaDuma cannot hide her anger as she finally arrives home. Priest sees, when she is close enough, that she has been crying. But MaDuma is not really crying for failing to get the potatoes. Priest knows his wife very well. She is crying because she has made a fool of herself.

This is bad indeed. Priest feels sorry for his wife, but there is nothing he can do. He stands outside for another hour, afraid to go inside and face her. As he stands there thinking about how things have changed for the worse when everybody thought they would change for the better, he sees two young boys of about eleven or twelve carrying around two kilograms of potatoes each. They must have followed the tractor to Mswane. Now they are not running; instead they are striding fast. Priest, like everybody who sees the boys, need not be told that the boys are happy.

"Who knows," Priest thinks, "maybe they did not have food this whole day. Or they ate pap without anything to help it down their throats." Priest thinks of the woman who passed here laughing and hopes that the children are hers. "That might stop her from laughing."

He smiles and goes inside.

After fourteen months the workers finish planting the number of trees Johnson wants. Priest, and many others, soon resume the title of being unemployed. All the months they have toiled at the farm comprised extreme suffering and torture to their bones and muscles. It became a little better when they started the actual planting, although the money was reduced. But now all is gone.

Things soon return to what they were. Although there was not a great difference while he was working at the farm, the family has been able to buy enough maize to see them through the month. Priest's children have known hunger for a long time now, yet they cannot get used to it. It is like death. Every time it hits is as bad as the first. But at least they are used to eating bad food.

"Mother sent me to ask for maize meal," a young girl says as Priest and his wife are seated in their living room, not talking to each other. As things have changed from bad to worse, the two parents find it hard to engage in a conversation without it ending in a fight.

As the young girl speaks, MaDuma looks askance at Priest, who, having heard the question, utters a big, "NO."

"Tell your mother we are sorry, we have no maize meal," MaDuma says sternly. "Father is not working at the farm any more, in case she has forgotten. We have nothing."

MaDuma is losing her temper speedily. How can anybody ask

from them in times like this when everybody has to hold on to the little they have?

The girl waits a little while, hoping to hear one of them remember that just this morning MaDuma bought 12.5 kilograms of maize meal. But, contrary to what the girl hopes, Priest earnestly confirms what his wife has said. "Tell your mother we are sorry that we cannot help her. Life is hard these days."

As the girl opens the door to leave, Priest decides to offer her some soothing words instead of the maize meal. "Tell your mother not to forget that God loves us, and He sees us."

The girl is annoyed by what Priest tells her after having just lied to her. "No Father, that is not true. There is no God."

The girl's words move Priest. Before he can find the words to refurnish the girl with her lost faith, she closes the door and leaves.

As soon as the girl is gone, Priest and MaDuma go to the kitchen where their maize is. They do not tell each other where they are going, so they only realise they are heading for the same place once they have arrived. The woman arrives first, and is very relieved to see their maize safe and sound. She opens the bag and says, "They are playing. They will not get you." MaDuma closes the paper bag and leaves, allowing Priest to utter his reassuring words to the maize meal.

But Priest does not go to the bag of maize meal with reassuring words in mind. He goes there with something different. He knows that no matter how much they save, their maize will sooner or later be finished. The bag of maize meal was opened this morning when MaDuma prepared the family something in between breakfast and lunch. This means it has been used once, but what Priest sees disturbs him so much that he forgets his rank in society.

"Dogs!" he curses. "The lazy dogs have no understanding of fullness. They are cheating us." Priest closes the bag angrily and leaves. He cannot believe this! These people are reducing the content in the bags while they increase prices.

When he arrives in the living room, he sees a figure distinct with anger standing next to the door. The figure is a woman's and she happens to be MakaNozipho, the mother of the girl who has just come to ask for maize meal. Priest is stupefied.

"I sent my daughter to ask for maize meal but she came back empty-handed," the figure speaks, trying in vain to look at both MaDuma and Priest at the same time. Failing this, she resorts to looking at them alternately. Priest and MaDuma do not know what to say, so they decide to keep quiet, allowing MakaNozipho a chance to continue. "I came to ask why that happened."

"We told her we have no maize meal," MaDuma says, as if having no maize meal is something to be proud of. She looks for confirmation from her husband, who gives it without hesitation.

MakaNozipho's face becomes darker when she hears another pair of lies directed at her ears. Priest only now notices that MakaNozipho has a large nose. It is moving up and down as if it has a life of its own. "You are lying!" she bursts out in anger. "You do have maize meal. You," she points a finger at MaDuma, "I saw you coming with it from Yizo-Yizo. You have it."

Priest and MaDuma look at each other in disbelief. MaDuma tried to avoid being seen in the morning, but she has certainly failed. She decides to say something quickly, lest her husband make a mistake. "Yes, it is true. You did see me come from Yizo-Yizo with maize meal. But it came when we owed so many people their maize that it got finished when we paid them back."

MaDuma looks at Priest, who feels obliged to nod approval and sends another surreptitious glance at MakaNozipho.

"You are lying!" MakaNozipho accuses again.

"I think it's time for you to leave our house," MaDuma shouts. "You have no right to come here and accuse us of lying. What we are telling you is true. So go!"

MakaNozipho does not move. MaDuma looks around for any object she may use if she needs force in order to get rid of this woman.

Instead of leaving, MakaNozipho speaks again. "You say you paid other people their maize meal. What about my own you borrowed when Priest had not even started working at the farm?"

Priest and his wife are very shocked when they hear this. Two years? They look at each other and then face MakaNozipho with the same question. MakaNozipho repeats herself in the same words but louder.

MaDuma gets angrier now. "This woman has come to rob us of our maize meal and I will not let that happen." She starts to sweat and breathe heavily. "From now on there will be no helping each other with maize meal, or anything for that matter. In times like this, the teachings of the Bible only count in the church, not outside."

She stops to regain her strength while Priest and MakaNozipho look at her, shocked.

"Jesus did not know that it would come to this, otherwise he wouldn't have said one should love one's neighbour as much as one loves oneself." Now MaDuma might cry at any minute. She is angry, confused and sorry. All in one. "No one can afford to love her neighbour these days. Not even half as much as she loves herself."

Priest looks at his wife and sees somebody he does not know. She never was a very kind person, but she has also never been like this. What has hunger done to his wife? Priest looks at MakaNozipho and sees that she, too, is shocked. All this time all the neighbouring families have shared in their suffering and want. Now everyone is on their own.

"Okay then," MakaNozipho starts in a calm voice, "you eat your maize meal forever. There will be no helping each other from now on." She bangs the door and leaves.

14

It is now five weeks after the cutting off of Muntukabani's testicles and three weeks after the same operation was performed on Dlamini. Nomsa cannot get either of these incidents out of her mind. Dlamini's case is difficult because he tried to fight and the Grinding Stone beat him severely before removing his genitals. The mutilation of the men affected Nomsa so much that now she cannot look at a man's trousers, especially the zip, without envisioning the blood that came out of both these men. She sees Muntukabani's penis becoming tumescent and then falling forever. She feels her scalp tingle when this happens and tries hard to remind herself that what they did was right. They are speaking for the women who cannot speak for themselves and they are using the only language men understand – violence.

Nomsa is grateful that she has a very good man who understands her. Who does not beat or abuse her because of her attitude towards pregnancy and sex.

It is a hot October Sunday and Nomsa opens the fridge to get some juice. She is so shocked by what she sees that she thinks she may be hallucinating. Inside the fridge are fifteen pairs of bulls' testicles arranged in three rows of five each. She feels a superstitious fear grip her as she notices that all the white balls are in the top row and the blacks in the middle, while the reds are at the bottom. Her first response to the sight is that it must have something to do with the cutting of

Muntukabani's and Dlamini's genitals. Again, Muntukabani's penis hardens and she tries hard not to scream.

It is her helper, Ntombi, who saves her by telling Nomsa that she has seen for herself Bongani coming in with the plastic bag full of "them" and putting them in the fridge.

"Oh my God! He is mad!" Nomsa says, and holds her mouth with the palm of her left hand. "What was he thinking, bringing this dirt to my house? My fridge?"

"It's hard to tell. But he looked very pleased as he kept arranging and rearranging them."

Nomsa's mouth is open as she listens.

"I heard him talk to himself about the joys of fatherhood and I asked him what he meant by that and he said it was so nice a book that I should read it."

"I can't believe this!" Nomsa does not know what to think. It is better that no ghost has brought these testicles, but knowing that Bongani has done it worries her. The only explanation for it is that he is mad, and she thinks about having a mad husband and decides that it is not a good thing. "He is mad!" she says again, as if saying it can reverse the condition.

"At least," Ntombi offers, "he sounded very happy. I have never seen him this happy before."

"Where is he?" Anger and fear are mingled in Nomsa's voice.

"In the toilet," Ntombi says, with a mouth full of a muffin she is eating with coffee, in spite of the heat.

"I've just been to the toilet and he is not there," Nomsa protests.

Ntombi takes a few seconds swallowing before she answers, "He said he will use the outside one because there is no privacy inside." Ntombi takes a sip of her coffee.

"He said what?" Nomsa does not await a reply. As she briskly strides outside, she opens her mouth and Ntombi notices her tongue moving in and out of the gap. She thanks God that Nomsa is not angry at her.

The toilet to which Nomsa is going is just a few metres from the house. It is very old but in a useable condition. It was erected many years ago when this home was built for some white family, but it has not been used since the Hadebe family was renting out the two outbuilding rooms. When they got so rich that they could build a double-storey and demolish the outbuilding, they kept the toilet to use in times of emergency, like when they have some function that brings many people together. This toilet is always locked, but Ntombi has been instructed to clean it at least once a month.

When Nomsa is close to the toilet, she remembers that a madman cannot be trusted, so she takes two steps back before she shouts, "Bongani, are you there?"

Instead of getting an answer, she hears Bongani groaning inside, "Oh my mother! Is that silly herbalist trying to kill me? Ohhh! Ouch! *Awe malo!*"

Nomsa waits for a few moments trying to hear what Bongani is saying, but her confusion dulls her ears. "Bongani, are you all right?"

Only now does Bongani hear her and cries loudly, "Ohhh! Leave me alone!"

Nomsa again asks what his problem is.

"It's beans!" Bongani is still in pain as he speaks.

Nomsa is completely lost as to what Bongani is talking about. She pushes the door forcibly and kicks it when she finds it locked. "What is wrong, Bongani? Open this door! Now!"

"It's beans. Oooo! Leave me alone, beans!"

When she hears this, Nomsa thinks her husband has been poisoned, and for a moment she forgets her anger about the bulls' testicles in her fridge and rushes to the garage in fright to start the car and take her husband to the hospital. She shouts at Ntombi to come and assist her quickly. It is better to have a poisoned husband than a mad one.

As Nomsa runs to get the car, Bongani is groaning and cursing Sgonyela. Then he hears his wife and Ntombi coming and starts groaning again, "Leave me alone, beans!"

"Where did you eat, Bongani?"

"At Zwelakhe's. Hmmn!" Bongani says without thinking. It is as if he has anticipated her.

"But I told you that they hate you, those people. Look now!"

Bongani drags himself out of the toilet and Nomsa and Ntombi help him to the car.

When they are about to reach the Central Hospital, Bongani is no longer groaning as much. Nomsa takes the opportunity to ask him why in hell did he bring "those" things to her house.

"What are testicles for?" Bongani answers. "There is only one biological function of testicles that I know of: to create something which, if pumped into something, creates something that I want."

"You are mad!" Nomsa yells at Bongani, and for a moment she forgets that she is driving and almost loses control of the car. "Would you stop talking in parables and answer my question?"

But then they arrive at the hospital and the matter is put aside for a moment. Nomsa makes arrangements with the nurses and clerks – many of whom live in Canaan and respect them – to let Bongani see the doctor before the people already waiting for the doctor to arrive. Because it is a Sunday, the doctor only comes when she has been called. The wait will be long, and Nomsa is in no mood for her mad husband, so she leaves him sitting on the bench, telling him to call her when he is done.

When the doctor finally arrives at quarter to twelve, Bongani is called to see her first. The other patients protest, but the nurse tells them that Bongani phoned early in the morning to make an appointment. He is indeed a VIP and is unlike them, who simply brought their big foreheads to the hospital without making an appointment.

Bongani does not know the name of his doctor and no one tells him, so he decides that she is a Chinese woman as young or as old as he is. When she asks him what his problem is, the best Bongani can say is, "It's beans."

For a while the doctor thinks maybe it is her poor English that makes her misunderstand or be misunderstood by Bongani. It is when she looks at the nurse and sees her smiling that she realises the problem may be with the answering, not her question.

"What I'm trying to say is, 'Where is the pain?'" she tries again.

"It's here," Bongani points to his posterior.

When he tells her this, the doctor takes a pen and hurriedly scribbles in Bongani's file. It is her day off, but she has many patients to see and so she is in a rush. "I think you have piles, Mr Hadebe. Take this to the dispensary and they will give you pills and painkillers. If that does not work, you will have to be operated on to have them removed."

As he stands up to leave, Bongani feels some strange movement in his anus. "Oh! My mother! They are starting again!" he tells the waiting patients and the walls of Out-patient Department.

He drags himself to the hall where the window to the dispensary is and seats himself in the queue. The ailment is not new to him. He started suffering from piles as a very young boy. He smiles as he recalls that he felt so special when he knew that he had an anus that nobody else had. He used to stoop, display his anus and push. When he did this, something came out from within and it was that which the people viewed and were pleased by. Not a day passed when Bongani was not asked to show his anus. Many times he even got paid for it. "Show us your anus, Bongani!" they used to say.

It was in the 1980s when he was in high school that he came to know the piles for what they were – painful and bleeding intruders. They almost killed him. He made an observation concerning them: The intruders were Satan's disease that could breathe on their own.

"Oh God, I am going to be lean again!" he laments aloud, and the man who is next to him laughs.

When he has finally got his prescriptions, he calls Nomsa from his cell phone to come and fetch him. He then moves slowly outside to wait for her. On the way out is a shop where he buys *The Eye of People*. He knows that Nomsa will not come right away, but will make a point of taking her time.

As he comes out of the gates, two boys run to him and tell him that if he is going to town, he should use the car that each is pointing to.

"No. Someone is coming to fetch me! Thanks."

"Shit!" one of the boys curses and leaves as the driver of the car hoots for him. The other goes inside to get two people who are coming from the hospital.

Bongani sits and reads without making any sense of what the stories he is reading are about. His mind is troubled that the disease from hell has attacked him again. It is on page three that he finds a face that catches his attention. Although at first he cannot place the man with a big head full of pimples, he soon sees that it is a man he has visited twice in a month and that the man is Sgonyela. It angers him that the medicine from this man whose photo is in front of him has caused the return of his disease from hell.

His anger increases when he reads that Sgonyela has been arrested in connection with the murder of an old man who lived somewhere around Manakanaka. The article continues that Sgonyela is also under investigation for other related crimes, such as killing people for body parts. The reporter suggests that these body parts are allegedly used by the popular herbalist to make medicine for many of his clients' needs.

"Bastard!" Bongani curses aloud. "My children? My money?"

"What children?" Nomsa asks from behind, and for a moment Bongani runs out of words. "What the hell are you talking about? Hhe, Bongani? Are you trying to tell me that you have children I do not know about?" Nomsa starts to feel hot. "Oh my God! What is happening to me? Why this now?"

"It's not like that. The thing is—"

"Shut up! You're lying about something!"

Bongani begs his wife to calm down and promises to tell her the whole story, which he does. He tells her how having children is so important to him, and what he has done to try to get them.

"Do you even love me?" she asks. "Or is all you care about children?"

"Of course I do! Why do you think I am still committed to you and don't have a child with someone else? You are so precious to me that I can't think of not creating this special thing with you. Children are a blessing."

Nomsa sits down beside her husband. "It is time that we are honest with each other. I will tell you the actual reason why I am resolved not to have children."

15

"For as long as I can remember, I have not been a complete person," Nomsa says. "There has always been a void in me and I want you to understand. Perhaps then I will be able to be a human being again. I always ask myself why the Living Ghost chose me? Maybe this is a question I will keep asking but will find no answer to.

"It all started when I was about six years old. I did not know what it was then. My father used to be so interested in me, offering to wash me and all. I did believe he loved me as he always said when he wanted to spend time with me. I remember that when he washed me, he took time touching my private parts. I did not worry too much because I did not know what it meant. Every time he got a chance he would offer to wash me. Even when I refused, saying that I could wash myself, he insisted. I think that Mother was pleased at first because she believed it proved that he loved me. This went on for a long time and I was getting used to it. Then he started to do other things. When he washed me, he would sit me on his lap, making sure that I touched his private parts.

"I was eight when he began to take out his penis. I remember that he used to let me sit with my legs wide open so my private parts touched his. I began to feel uneasy about this. As young as I was I just knew that something was wrong about what he did to me. What worried me even more, though, is that it felt good when he did it. Even today I still hate myself for ever feeling like that.

"He would always stop once he had peed on me, though of course it wasn't really pee. It just seemed that way because I was so young. I could see that every time he peed he changed, becoming agitated and afraid. I started to hate and fear him. He told me that what he did was our special secret. I was not supposed to tell anyone. I was not supposed to tell, even in my dreams.

"But the worst was yet to come. I was ten when I told my mother that I did not want my father to wash me any more. She asked me why and I did not tell her the truth. I said I was grown enough to wash myself. When Mother told him to not wash me any more, I could see that he was really angry. But he pretended he was only disappointed because he was trying to help me. Our relationship started to be tenser now. He knew I said what I said because I knew what he did to me was wrong.

"Then one day he came to my room. I could tell by the look in his eyes that something was really amiss. There was something evil on his mind. At first he started by trying to be nice, telling me that he loved me very much. He said I was his favourite little girl and I would always be special to him. It was a hot day and I was only wearing a light skirt with nothing on top. After going on about his love for me, he started to touch me, trying to get my skirt off at the same time. I began to cry and told him to leave me alone. Now he had become a fearsome person who looked like a stranger to me. I thought the devil had taken over. I cried even louder and soon realised that it was useless because there was nobody home who could hear me. The devil had chosen his timing perfectly. I tried to push his hands off me but he was too strong. He managed to put his hands under my panties while he held me down with his other hand. He kept telling me that it was okay. He was not going to hurt me. I struggled until I completely ran out of strength. He took off my pants and … all I can say is the man killed me that day.

"When he was finished he told me not to tell anyone. I told him I was going to tell Mother, but he said she would not believe me, nobody would believe a lying little whore like me. I told him to go to hell, but he laughed at me, saying he would gladly go when the time was right. I was hurt and hopeless. He knew that he had won and so he kept doing it whenever he felt like it or got a chance.

"One day I did tell Mother but, as he had said, she did not believe me. She went to ask him if it was true and he said I was crazy, that I hated him and so I was making up lies about him. She only believed my story when I was fourteen and got pregnant. I could see that she was hoping I would say I had had sex with another boy, but I kept telling her that it was him. My father was the father of the child I was carrying. She then suggested we get rid of the baby, which we did. It was after that that I vowed never to have a child again. In honour of my dead baby."

"But you should have told me," Bongani says. "I would not have pushed you and tried all these ploys to get children. If I had known all of this I would have been a different man towards you."

As they drive back home Nomsa is silent, thinking about what Bongani has told her about Sgonyela's medicines. Can that black medicine really work? Can it be the reason for the dreams she has been having? Dreams of her unborn baby, begging her to be taken home. Can it be the reason for the nausea she has been feeling in the mornings recently?

She recalls a story her grandmother told her about a couple who consulted an *inyanga* when they were unable to have children. As a result, they got a son who turned out to be something very scary. At the age of six months he started to steal raw meat and eat it. When they went to ask the *inyanga* what was wrong with the baby he told them that he had given them one of his children – one who had become a problem for him. The *inyanga* told them not to complain. They had asked for a child and he had given them one.

Nomsa is worried. Will whatever is growing inside her be human or will it be something created by Sgonyela's potions?

16

"Here is your supper, my husband. Please enjoy yourself," MaDuma says as she places the tray on the coffee table. Priest feels happy when he sees his food. He is tired. He has been working all day planting in his garden. "Thank you. You do not know how hungry I am," he says and takes away the plate covering his food. His face changes when he sees that it is only pap.

"You are making a fool out of me!" Priest shouts, gesturing with his open hand at the food.

"Oh! My God! Didn't I bring a glass of water?" MaDuma comes back to look at her husband's food. "But it's here," she says coolly.

"You mean water?"

"Yes, Sandile's father. I thought you would use it to help your food down. There is no other way." MaDuma seats herself on another sofa, across from her husband. "Eat *uphuthu* and drink water. And enjoy." She smiles.

"You continue mocking me?" Priest is now pitch black with anger.

"Getting angry with me will not help at all, Sandile's father. Just imagine chicken when you eat. This is hunger. It is powerful."

The following day Priest goes to search for work at the "courthouse". This is an abandoned building that was used many years ago by the people of Ndlalidlindoda to prosecute the criminals in the area when the residents had had enough of crime and the police were not helping. He arrives at about half past eight. Many people are already here. Some are standing across the road, near Ntuli's spaza shop. They look at the faded sign above the courthouse: "Jealous Down Butchery". Underneath are the words "Pork full of surprises", which tells everyone who sees it that, in its day, this butchery had served pork lovers quite well.

Priest goes inside the courthouse, which no longer has windows or doors. It is empty, except for two large tables. It shows that the place has not been used in a long time. Everything is dirty and covered with dust. On top of one table are coils of human excrement.

Once everybody has arrived, the job begins. Now the table that has no faeces is taken outside and three men stand over it and face the others. Bongani, who is in charge of Community Development in Gxumani, has some papers in front of him. He hits the table lightly with his hands and announces loudly, "Now, people, listen carefully. I want you to know that we cannot possibly employ all of you as you are so many. Even the grass is not as many as you are."

Priest feels a pang in his heart as the people laugh at the joke. He can always feel if things are not going to be okay for him. His gut tells him that he is not going to get the job as a road digger.

"A person will be employed because of his luck," Bongani starts after the laughter has ceased. "We give everybody a chance. So we have decided to give you numbers. If your number is called, you will get the job. If it is not, at least you will have it to yourself." Bongani smiles again. The seekers of employment are too frightened to laugh now. The moment of truth has come.

A man goes around with a bucket and everyone picks a piece of paper out of it. Priests' number is 107.

"I think we should start with prayer," Priest suggests humbly. "I don't feel confident at all. I always feel like this when I am going to lose."

"You want us to pray for you?" one woman shouts at Priest. "You are crazy! Can't you see that if you lose it will be better because our chances will increase?"

"Okay, people!" Bongani intervenes. "You don't have to argue now. Everybody close your arses tightly as now I am calling the lucky numbers."

But Bongani is interrupted by another loud, hoarse voice that is not directed at him. "You, beautiful Thembuz of Gubazi. You, who awaited the dog to give birth so that you will eat sour milk."

Everybody looks in the direction of the man, Sithole. He is talking to his ancestors and he does not give a damn about other people. "Here I am," he continues. "I ask you, grandmother Nomsompiya, to go to that man and fetch this number 38 I am holding here. If I am not employed today, it will mean you do not exist!" he says sternly. The others laugh. Sithole pays no heed to them. "Ha! I have been slaughtering goats and cattle and nothing happens!"

After ten minutes the people at the courthouse are divided into two groups. Those whose numbers have been called stand on the slope to the left of the building. Priest is among those who were unlucky. They are still standing where they were, facing the employers across the table. Priest looks at Sithole and smiles. His grandmother did not come to pick the number 38 for him.

"As I have told you," Bongani says, "we cannot employ all of you at the same time. Those who failed today will get employed in future. There is still so much to be done. We are still to build more roads and bridges, and many other things."

"I think there is a mistake here, Bhungane," interrupts the loud voice of a short, dark man. Bongani looks at him, astonished. Many people know the man. He is Sokhela.

"There is a number you have forgotten. You left out number 14 by mistake. Can you search for it in your pockets?" Sokhela shouts. He is in the group of the unemployed but is not as worried as they are. The noise of disbelief stirs among the people:

"What is this man saying?"

"Isn't he mad?"

"Are you talking, my brother?" Bongani asks.

"I was saying that you did not call all the numbers. Number 14 was mistakenly left out." Sokhela sounds sincere.

Bongani recognises him and frowns. He tries successfully to hide his shock, and shouts, "I don't understand what you are talking about!"

"It's me," Sokhela says. "I was at your house yesterday. Don't you remember the 'short-cut' prayer?"

"Did you or did you not smoke today?" Bongani asks in a loud voice.

"I didn't smoke. I am perfectly fine."

"Can somebody who has dagga help this man."

Other people laugh. Sokhela is on the verge of crying now.

Bongani does not notice Sokhela's anger. "He is craving for dagga – now his mind is not working straight."

The listeners laugh again.

Priest goes back home with Sithole. Sithole lives at Phanekeni, a little further from Priest's home. On their way they talk about their situation. They both have left their families in bad conditions. Food is scarce in their homes. Priest tells Sithole that he is even afraid of going home to his wife. The two men also speak about Sokhela. Sithole tells Priest that Sokhela is not mad at all. In fact, Bongani has also told him about the short-cut prayer Sokhela spoke about. The principal came to him, Sithole, and told him that if he gave him R200, he would be employed. But Sithole refused, relying on his ancestors instead.

When he arrives home, Priest expects to see his wife angry, but she is not. As soon as he has sat down on the sofa, MaDuma enters the living room and takes her seat. She does not ask how it went at the courthouse. She needs no telling. She observes him and then asks, "Is it true that you have been without a job for six years now, Sandile's father?"

"No. Five years and four months. In fact four years if you count my working days at the farm."

"Whatever."

"I think this is Satan's doing. He is tempting us. He wants to see how much we love our God."

MaDuma's voice is calm. "I have made up my mind. I am going to see the sangoma."

"You know that I am a priest, MakaSandile. How can you do such a thing?"

"I will do it," MaDuma's voice is low. She is determined.

"MakaSandile, please!" Priest starts to beg. He knows that if his wife has set her mind on something then nothing can stop her. "What are people going to say?"

"I don't care what people say. In times like this," she starts sternly, "one needs things that are tangible."

"Oh God! I am not going to be promoted to a bishop."

MaDuma leaves the following morning. Because she has no money to pay for a taxi, she walks. She leaves home at about six and arrives at Khumalo's at half past seven. Khumalo is a Zionist. He is a healer who uses both herbs and holy water. He prays to Jesus and the ancestors. His home is situated near Juteni Road at Ndlangamandla. He has a big white house and a short kneel-and-pray hut, which he uses for consultation.

When she arrives, MaDuma is tired. She goes to sit on a bench in front of the house. There is a young lady already sitting here. She tells MaDuma that there is somebody inside. As they speak, the door opens and another woman comes out. The one who is on the bench stands to leave and MaDuma realises the two women are leaving together.

When she is called to enter, MaDuma spends a minute admiring the room she has entered. The floor is plastered and anointed with red polish. There are two calabashes where Khumalo is kneeling. On his right there are different herbs that MaDuma does not know. She likes the smell in the room.

Khumalo is wearing a gold shawl with black spots, the colour of a tiger. He burns the incense when MaDuma has told him she wants him to foretell for her.

"Hhethe!" Khumalo sneezes.

"We agree!" MaDuma says loudly.

"I see suffering!"

"We agree!"

"I see the father of the home is in trouble."

"We agree!"

"I see his head almost breaking in pain."

MaDuma keeps quiet.

"No. It's work. He needs work!"

"We agree."

"Hhethe!"

"Great Kings."

MaDuma arrives home in the afternoon. She is hungry, tired and angry. She knows there is no food so she does not bother to go to the kitchen. Instead, she goes to her bedroom and locks herself inside, having told her husband that she is not to be disturbed. She wants to take a nap to clear her head because what Khumalo told her disturbs her very much. At first she decides not to tell her husband, but then she changes her mind. Now she is sleeping to gather her strength.

It is exactly ten past five in the afternoon when MaDuma wakes up and goes to join her husband in the living room. Priest is watching the Siswati news on SABC1. But what he likes more is about to begin. Being unemployed has caused Priest to have more time to himself than he wants. As a member of the unemployed community, Priest has developed a great interest in watching soap operas, especially the one that is about to show – *Days of Our Lives*.

MaDuma seats herself on the sofa and keeps quiet. Three minutes pass and nobody says a word to the other. MaDuma goes to the television set and chokes it off. It is old and the two parts are balanced against each other. Although there is an old wall unit in the house, the television is placed on a sofa, to make it "comfortable", as Priest always says.

MaDuma goes back to her seat and says nothing. Priest smiles to himself when he realises his wife is hunting for a fight. He is not about to give in to her whims so easily. Two more minutes pass and nobody says a word. It is as though they are in some kind of a competition in which whoever speaks first will lose. MaDuma has won once, when she turned off the television. But she wants to win again and again and again.

When these two parents were still so deeply in love, they used to play a "gazing game" in which they looked at each other closely without uttering a sound. If one of them laughed, the other would win. MaDuma wanted them to always play this game because she always won and she liked winning. As time progressed, she forced her husband to bet when they played. Whoever lost, which always happened to be Priest, would buy a drink for the other. Sometimes they bought the drink before the game began. If this was done, MaDuma insisted on buying Coke because it was her favourite and she knew she would win.

Priest used to tell his wife that he could not help smiling when he looked at her like that because she was so beautiful. MaDuma was really flattered by this. But in reality, Priest has an easy smile. He has a sense of humour. Until a few years ago, it was hard, or even impossible, for Priest to look at his image in the mirror and not smile. When MaDuma learnt that her husband smiled when he looked at himself as well, she was angry. She wanted her face to be the only one that made him smile.

"This is tantamount to masturbation," she growled at Priest when she finally caught him. "You know that masturbation is a sin."

It's eighteen minutes past five now and MaDuma finally decides that she is not going to win this one. She wants to tell Priest about her journey. She clears her throat twice and looks for a smile on Priest's face. There is none. There is neither smile nor anger. He is absolutely expressionless. MaDuma cannot hold herself any longer: "Okay! You win."

"I win what?"

"The battle. What else?"

"Ohho!" Priest waves a dismissive hand at his wife.

MaDuma pauses and then says, "Khumalo says you won't get a job because you are bewitched."

"You see? I told you that sangomas tell lies," Priest says triumphantly.

"Listen to me, will you!" MaDuma says sternly. "He said they bewitched you to be disagreeable with the oils of a wild pig, now your blood is not flowing." She pauses. She wants to take her time. "And he is right, you know. I have always wondered why I sometimes hate you so much." MaDuma waits for her husband to speak but he doesn't. She carries on, "I think you will have to see him and get some herbs."

Priest is shocked. "What?"

"I am saying," MaDuma shouts, "you should go to Khumalo so that he will clean your blood and free you of the evil spirit." Then she laughs. "Shit! I almost forgot. He said they bewitched you with the female tokoloshe when you were young and she is growing with you. Sis!" She spits on the floor. "That is why my body is always so weak. It's the jealousy of this woman of yours."

MaDuma is angry now. Priest can see the sweat sparkling on her face and nose, especially her nose. "I have always wondered why you sleep as flat as you do. You are having fun with your lover."

Priest is speechless as he watches his wife wipe the sweat flowing down to her neck. He does not believe what he has just heard. Not that he did not expect such nonsense from a seer, but he never thought that his wife would believe it. When MaDuma has finished mopping her face and neck and her breathing speed has returned to normal, Priest asks her, "Do you believe all this nonsense, MakaSandile?"

"Of course I do," MaDuma responds readily. "He said something I can see with my own eyes – that your blood is stagnant! If it is not, then where do you work?"

"This is crazy!" Priest is angry now. "How can I live if my blood is not flowing?"

"The question is," MaDuma starts defiantly, "the question is how do you live as your blood is not flowing? The answer is that I do not want to know!" MaDuma feels deep satisfaction when she sees Priest blink repeatedly. He is on the verge of crying. She has won. She pushes on the television and is pleased to see her favourite character: Stefano DiMera!

Priest leaves his wife, but has no idea where he is going. He just wants to be away from MaDuma and her nonsense. It is one thing for her to go to the seer, but it is crazy to think that he, a man of God, can go to the sangoma and use his medicine. No. He is a priest and he wants to be promoted to a bishop. How can he become a bishop if he visits sangomas? People who are destined to go to hell? No ways!

Priest decides to visit his friend Sithole at Phanekeni. As he walks, he thinks about how the land he lives in is deteriorating economically. Things are getting worse as more and more people lose their jobs and come to add to the number of the unemployed at Hunger-Eats-a-Man. Two big stores, Intuthuko Store and Mpumalanga Market, could not hold out against the depression. These are the oldest stores in Hunger-Eats. They have been great in their time. Now Intuthuko Store has closed completely, while Mpumalanga Market is still trading, although it is clear to everyone that the owners are losing their battle dismally.

Across the road, on the left if you come to Hunger-Eats-a-Man from Blood River, there is a spaza shop that many think has helped to bring about the downfall of Mpumalanga. Sinethemba Spaza Shop, as it is called, is now the main trader in groceries in the Manhlanzini and Mafikeni sections. It always fascinates Priest how suddenly everybody goes to Sinethemba without even thinking about Mpumalanga, which was so great in its time. He is guilty of it too. Two months previously, when he wanted to post a letter, he went to Sinethemba to buy the stamp and then went to the postbox, which is outside Mpumalanga. He hated himself later for doing this. Why didn't he buy his stamp from Mpumalanga? The next time he needed to post a letter, he made a point of going to buy the stamp at Mpumalanga. But when he saw how empty it was, he realised there were many chances that there would be no stamps there. To avoid disappointing the lady who ran the store and hurting himself for doing it, he decided to ask for anything he could see. "Can I have one pack of King Kong, please!" he had said. There was no beer being brewed at his home, but sorghum was the only thing that caught his eye.

It takes Priest about eight minutes to arrive at Sithole's home. There are two buildings at Sithole's. The five-roomed house is near the gate while the rondavel is on the other end. Priest knocks at the living-room door after bracing himself for what he will see inside, or what he will not see. Sithole is in so much debt that he has lost all his living-room furniture. He borrowed money from the stokvel and could not pay it back. The women of the stokvel came to claim his furniture when they realised Sithole was unable to pay. By now the money he owed has multiplied greatly. Money borrowed in this fashion is generally called *mashonisa*, but some call it *zaliwe* because it can give birth. It is also called *zanxapha* (click-of-annoyance), because people are always angry when they pay double what they borrowed. But Priest prefers to call it "give birth and multiply rapidly", a phrase he has borrowed from the Old Testament.

As Priest enters, Sithole is seated on a bucket that is turned upside down. His wife, MaXulu, is seated on the bench near the door. "Here is a person, Sithole," she says.

"I see him," Sithole responds sternly.

"It's Father Gumede, Sithole, don't say you see him!"

"Now what do you want me to do? Lick him because it's Gumede?"

"Tell him to sit!"

When Priest has sat down on the bench beside MaXulu, all three in the room feel comfortable. It doesn't matter that there is no furniture. They talk about many things. They blame their leaders for not doing enough to help the common people.

Two hours pass in this fashion before Priest announces that he is leaving.

"Thank you for visiting us," Sithole says kindly.

Priest's voice and face change as he says, "You don't even have water in this house?" Priest looks at Sithole and MaXulu alternately. "I came here a long time ago and you have offered me nothing!"

Sithole smiles. "But you did not tell us that you are thirsty." He looks at his wife, who reads the unpronounced command and heads for the kitchen, only to be interrupted by the men's conversation when she is halfway.

"Water is what we have," Sithole smiles again.

"I am not talking about 'pure' water!" Priest says calmly. "It's clear that you are a pagan Job of Matshana. It is not right for the representative of God to leave your house without even drinking tea when he has come to visit you. The angel that is responsible for planning my journeys will be angry. This will make that angel prevent me from visiting you again, saying you kill it with hunger."

"Did you come here to visit or to eat?" Sithole shouts.

"That question of yours is meaningless, Sithole," Priest says loudly. "Do you think I could come all this way for nothing? No, Sithole! Don't play like that."

"You came all this way to waste my children's food? *Cha-ke*! You won't get it. Now it is not like when I was driving at Putco and earning a good salary there." Sithole laughs and then continues, "Now a person who visits me should bring his lunch box if he likes."

"You are mad!" Priest bellows. "I'll rather not come at all."

"It's your choice."

17

"The time is nigh," the Book of God proclaimed many years ago. It still does. It is referring to the time when the Kingdom of God will come and His will shall be done on earth as in heaven. But occupying Priest's mind as he utters the words is something different. He is meditating on occurrences in his community and the fact that towards the end of the year the kingdom of some people on earth will be strengthened in the local elections. Fat cats like Hadebe will be voted to yet higher reaches, while those who vote them in will plunge further down into the pits.

Still ruminating on the elections, he recalls with wonder the enthusiasm and glee that characterised many blacks as they went to cast their first votes ever. So many people who voted! So many hopes shattered! That is why it came as no surprise at all that many people lost interest in the same liberating process five years later. Was it a realisation that voting did not guarantee a better life no matter who you voted for?

Some still held the right to vote very high:

"You must vote. It's your democratic right."

"You must vote to ensure that you play your part in putting the right government in place."

But others argued that a vote was meaningless:

"The most important democratic right for me is the right not to vote. What is the point in voting if you know all the candidates are only bent on bettering their own lives and empowering their relatives at the expense of all?"

"You should not talk like that. People will hear you," some replied. "And then you will no longer get your pension."

Even in the remote places like Skebhe and Place of Power people knew well the necessity of talking in whispers about the election:

"We must tell our children to vote, my husband. You know that this is the chief's land. If he says we must vote, then we must."

"What if our children go there and vote for the Xhosas, people who are not of our tribe?"

"Our chief is IFP. If he says we must vote for the IFP, then we must do just that."

"They will be fools to vote for somebody who does not belong to us. We were taught very well how to vote."

"Yes. We must put a cross next to a small elephant."

"Exactly."

That was back in 1999, but Priest is certain that those feelings have not dwindled over the years. If anything, they have escalated. More than ever, feelings of fear and distrust are dominating people's minds when it comes to politics. In fact, Priest recalls a man from one of those upper regions, Place of Power to be precise, who lost his life because he happened to be at the wrong place at the wrong time.

If he remembers correctly, the man had been in exile for many years, but when they were allowed back he did not come home. He stayed in the city. The place of his birth and his family and friends, where his umbilical cord was buried, had become the land of his enemies. This place where he had grown up shepherding his father's cattle, engaging in stick fights and fisticuffs with his mates.

Place of Power was famous for its peace and tranquillity, while other places were torn by internal violence between members of different political parties. But this tranquillity was tested when the exile's umbilical cord began to pull him to his birthplace despite his family's warnings that his birthplace need not become his death place as well.

Everybody was aware of the tantalising stories of a hero who had been in exile for years and returned to his place of birth where everybody had married with the enemy. Who did not know that the hero of the Nation's Spear was allowed three days of quietude by the leaders of the other party before they paid him a visit? It was certainly not an amicable welcome because the three strongly built men of the party had their rifles hanging threateningly on their shoulders as they went to greet the prodigal son of the land. It was not amusing to the party men that the sheep that was lost and found was as fearless as ever.

"Long time no see," one of the rifle-holders said foolishly, when the ritual of greeting had passed. Only then did they realise they were not quite sure how to say what they wanted to say to him.

"Yes. It's been a long time," the Nation's Spear responded. It was only the four of them at the Spear's home. These men had known one another well when they were boys growing up, but now they had become strangers.

An awkward hiatus lasted for a full minute and then one of the three party men reconnected with his vocabulary. "You know that things have changed around here since you have gone?"

"I know that, but I do not know how it concerns me," the Spear said without care. "I don't have a problem that you have chosen your way."

Another troubling pause.

"We came to tell you that if you want to stay here, you will have to join the party." This was the deputy chair who spoke. It's been years since the incident but nobody forgets that on that day his mouth was triple its size due to a lump on the inside of his lower lip. It was a difficult job for him to speak. It was therefore doubly annoying to hear his audience respond with a wild laugh.

The grass, the earth, the fences and the walls that were listening did not hear what happened next. Except that the Spear said some strange words and the three men left with their tails between their legs. The Spear said: "I don't like to be provoked, especially if those who provoke me are unarmed."

This had a weakening impact on the party men. They had gone there knowing quite well that their target was a trained soldier and only God knew what kinds of tricks these soldiers learnt in all the countries they went to. The men had expected he might want to give them some coins that might metamorphose into destructive bombs and blow them up. Their friends had carefully and worriedly warned them, "Don't touch anything he offers to you."

"Yes. And, please, no handshakes." Anything was possible with these defiers of death.

"Just hold on to your guns."

"If he tries anything stupid, shoot him!"

Even so, the Nation's Spear had described them as unarmed, and somehow they felt like they were indeed. It was like their guns had gone from their arms to the unarmed man.

All these thoughts invade Priest's mind as he considers the strangeness of our democracy and freedom. Now that the elections are near, our leaders remember that we are indispensable participants in the Rainbow Nation. That is why so many things are being promised and done for the people who have less to gain from the outcome of the elections. That is why today the Premier of the Province is coming to Bambanani High School to ceremoniously present computers to the school. It is a way of opening people's eyes to the diligence of those they have voted for and to make them see clearly that there is no other party worth their sacred crosses than the ruling party.

Priest spent time disputing within himself whether to go or not. Now he has decided and is unsure whether or not to honour the occasion with his priestly regalia. Not wearing his priestly garb will help if he is to be invisible, as he wants to be, but the problem is that he also knows that the regalia will come in handy since the main cause for his going there is to get food. Being identified as a respected priest will make his life easier when food is served. He decides to go without the priestly wear. If he gets the food, he will get it as the ordinary man he is.

Priest arrives at Bambanani High and is greeted by the pathetic bodies of the starving people from Hunger-Eats-a-Man roaming about near the tall gates of the school. A plethora of cars decorates the space between the main road and the school's tall fences. Inside the school premises teachers' and politicians' cars occupy different spaces and somehow it is clear which group owns which cars. The principal has obviously realised that his car is misplaced in its original parking space and has opted to move it to a space reserved for the politicians. "Funny guy," Priest thinks.

The Premier's silver-grey Mercedes-Benz C-Class is parked nearest to the tent erected for the VIPs. Just behind it is the black Volvo of the Minister of Transport, who is also the Master of Ceremonies. There are many other fancy cars and it pains Priest to look at them.

He proceeds to take his seat in an open space where chairs have been arranged to face the VIPs who are seated in the tent. He smiles within himself when he supposes that the main reason all these people have come is for the food. There is going to be plenty of it. They all know. Seven oxen have been slaughtered for the occasion. From all over the region people have come in large numbers. There are not enough seats for everyone. The students are forced to stand as more and more people keep flocking in.

Priest's eyes steal to the VIPs and his mouth is watering when he sees glasses of orange juice and saucers filled to the brim with snacks and sweets. The only thing available to Priest's group is the sweltering sun.

"Can you tell those ladies with umbrellas that we also want to see our leaders," one man announces, loud enough for the MC to catch his words. The MC pleads with the ladies who are trying to shield themselves from the scorching sun. The man who voiced his complaint is gratified when he learns how effective his words have been. So good to live in this new democracy where people's voices are heard!

"We too have our umbrellas," the complainant starts gleefully, "but we closed them for the sake of those behind us, who also have a democratic right to see their leaders. The Premier is like a father to us; we don't want to know him from TV screens only. We deserve a clear view." Although the man continues, the ladies have long since closed their umbrellas.

The MC is a light-complexioned man of about forty-one. Born and brought up here in Ndlalidlindoda, he now lives in a suburb in Durban. A graduate of Bambanani High, the MC's presence is a great inspiration to many attendants. He is now a respected member of the Provincial Parliament and, indeed, living proof that there is education in Bambanani after all. If education at Bambanani is poor then why did Philani Zondo make it to the top?

The MC commences by greeting and welcoming everyone, starting with the Premier and his delegates. He follows by greeting all the teachers and all the people of Ndlalidlindoda who are in attendance, congratulating the people in particular for their love and interest in the education of their children and the betterment of their community.

"Today we have yet again demonstrated to you that we are not the kinds of politicians who divorce themselves from the communities. Our Premier, when he came from Cape Town in 1996 to take up his honourable position, urged us all to come out of our offices and attend to the people's needs and wants." The MC pauses and women seize the opportunity to ululate. "It's sad that our country suffers great unemployment. We have come with these computers to help the youth and the community at large to empower themselves in the face of unemployment."

Different forms of applause follow this.

"Most of our youth are jobless because they lack the right skills required in the job market, and this offering of computers will render them employable in the government sector."

Utterances of "Hmn!", "That's true!" and "Yes!" greet this observation.

The MC decides to leave the thorny issue of unemployment because the Premier, who is the guest speaker, will tackle it in detail. He now cheers the people by singing the party slogan and offering some prizes in the form of party T-shirts with the Premier's face on the front. At the back of the T-shirts is printed: "Vote for the Man You Can Trust."

"What did the Premier say we should do when he took office in 1996?" the MC asks, as always punctuating his words with laughter.

Many people raise their hands and the MC opts for a boy towards the far end of the common people, next to the principal's office. "He said we should believe in Jesus Christ because he is the only one who died for our sins."

Other people laugh and the MC frowns, thinking the little brat is making a fool out of him. But he changes when he realises that the boy is mentally challenged. "I think we should give him a T-shirt," he says, and laughs.

The boy takes the T-shirt, smells it and then smiles. He then looks at the Premier's image on the T-shirt and at the man in front of him in great wonder. "I love this party!" the boy announces, and waves the T-shirt in the air as he goes to resume his seat. His action is greatly applauded on both sides.

The MC continues after the applause has subsided. "It is imperative that you people should remember that we are doing all this because you voted for us." He stops to laugh. "I always wonder what the people who did not vote for us say when they see us doing all these great things and those they voted for do nothing." Applause and ululation interrupt him. "Look at these roads we have built and upgraded! Look at the crèches and the taxi rank!"

Priest struggles not to say that he thinks the erection of the taxi rank at this time when people are dying of hunger is the most asinine thing their leaders have ever done. When they first heard about the creation of the taxi rank Priest had remarked, "The claims that these people are morons is very true. Only people who cannot think would do this."

"Why don't they use the money to create jobs for the poor? Or help people do things to make ends meet?" MaDuma had asked angrily of Priest, as if it were all his fault.

"I think they are too busy driving fancy cars to remember that there are some people who live in abject poverty. Or maybe they do not care," Priest had answered his wife.

When Priest's mind returns to the present, the Premier is about to give his address and everybody rises in honour of him. Priest, and a few people as dissatisfied as he is, do not stand up. The Premier may be rich and powerful, but he is not more human than Priest and everybody else. Besides, he is where he is because of these people's votes.

In his address, the Premier itemises the unfortunate happenings in the country, not failing to brag about his party's greatness in bringing the computers to the school. "Many of our youth are without employment because they are computer illiterate. Today we have made it possible for them to learn new skills that they otherwise would have been forced to go without." The Premier pauses, and the people applaud when they see he is asking for it. "A number of colleges are closing down because those who graduated from them cannot find jobs, especially those with education qualifications. Ezakheni College of Education has closed down, Mpumalanga College of Education has closed down, Esikhawini College of Education has closed down ..."

People get themselves involved by murmuring, "Hmn!", "Ohh Hhe!" and "*Awu Nkosi!*"

"This means people who were teaching in these institutions lost their jobs."

As Priest listens, he is amazed by the fact that the Premier is only listing the problems facing the country, without any suggestions in terms of solutions. "*Uyacula!*" – he is singing! – he says to himself.

"Many people wrongly believe that the government has got piles of money waiting to be distributed to people. Unfortunately, it is not like that. I should know. I am from there." The Premier smiles and common men and women clap their hands and laugh at his joke.

Even Priest cannot help laughing. His eyes dash to the fancy cars and words slip out of his mouth, "No. There is money. It's just that you do not keep it in piles but divide it among yourselves to use for your personal gain." Fortunately, he is not heard by the leaders and the party fanatics, otherwise something bad would happen to him.

After this Priest gets bored of listening and the sweltering sun, so he decides to go outside and join the many who have opted to hear no more of the Premier's speech. He is lucky to find an abandoned chair under a tree. As he sits there, he is able to hear only the ululation and the clapping from the dedicated followers. Just then he notices two young men holding one sheep each. The principal appears behind them, followed by the Minister and the representative of the company that donated the second-hand computers. When Priest hears that the sheep are to be given to these two rich people to take home and make themselves soup, Priest decides he has seen and heard enough. He even loses his appetite and leaves, muttering, "Our country is mad! Nothing is sane in our country!"

18

"I only wish we had another child younger than Zandi," MaDuma tells her husband as they are seated in front of their house.

Priest cannot believe his wife. "What? You wish we had another child? Another mouth to feed on nothing? No. Say you are joking."

"If we had another child younger than Zandi, we would get R200 every month."

"What?" Priest's face betrays confusion. "What are you talking about?"

"For a long time now people have been getting money for free from the government. The government gives R100 for every child under the age of seven, if the parents of that child are unemployed, like we are. So, you see, if we had another young child it would be R200." MaDuma cannot hide her happiness.

"Is this another of these people's lies?" Priest asks.

"It is true." MaDuma removes her eye-glasses and places the half-finished beadwork she is making on the coffee table. "I have spoken to many women who have actually got the money. Tomorrow, I'm going to register Zandi. R100 for free is better than nothing."

"Yes. It is indeed better than nothing," Priest agrees.

"It would have been better if Zandi had a twin sister or brother," MaDuma keeps thinking about the ways to increase their prospective earning. But she knows that nothing can be done. "At least we can hope we will get the R100," she adds.

"Hope!" Priest exclaims. "How long has one hoped for the things that do not happen? I wish there was a better word than hope. I hate to hope."

The sound of his voice tells MaDuma that he has already lost hope. This frightens her. "If you lose hope," she starts in a trembling voice, "I will not be able to get things done tomorrow. You must have hope!"

MaDuma leaves early the next morning, armed with all the documents she has been told are required for her purpose. She has the birth certificate of Zandi, her own and her husband's IDs, and the proof of her husband's unemployed status – the unemployment card. She arrives at the Welfare Department at about half past six. She is amazed to see so many people already waiting outside the building.

"Did you people sleep here or what?" MaDuma demands jokingly from the people. They range from old women to young girls of about twenty onwards. Many young girls have two children, one on their backs and the other walking on his or her own. Some who have mothers or grandmothers to look after their children have not brought them along. They have all come to register for the "money of the spinal cord", as the grant is referred to.

When MaDuma asks her question, many simply laugh. But one woman, who is huge and shapeless, with a big, almost four-cornered stomach, takes offence. The woman is about sixty years old or more. She seems to have had a beautiful face as a young girl, but her good looks are disturbed by her legs, which get thinner towards her ankles, ending in quite large feet. She is eating a fat cake for breakfast. When she hears MaDuma's joke she tries to swallow everything that is inside her mouth, which is much, but in vain. Her food is not well chewed so it cannot pass through the pharynx. She is choking. Her eyes look as if they will come out of their sockets. It takes about a minute before the fat cake is finally released down its path, thus rendering the woman able to speak and breathe freely. By this time everybody has forgotten what MaDuma said when she arrived. But the fat woman hasn't.

"You," the fat woman points at MaDuma. Her arm seems quite small on her huge body. "You have nearly killed me!"

Everybody is astonished by what the fat woman is saying. MaDuma has just arrived so how could she have tried to kill her? Is this some family feud or matter of their neighbourhood?

MaDuma is even more perplexed. This may be a case of mistaken identity. "I beg yours?" she asks. "I don't even know you."

"Don't say you beg mine," the old woman says angrily. "You almost killed me with your uncircumcised tongue."

"I still don't follow you. Speak Zulu, old lady!"

The fat lady starts angrily, "When you came here, you insulted us, thus causing my fat cake to choke me." She is trembling with rage now.

"Ohho! I thought you were talking. Somebody show Magogo where the toilet is. She needs to fart. *Uphisiwe*," MaDuma laughs and turns her head away from the fat woman, who tries to get up and charge towards MaDuma, but her health fails her.

"I wish you do not succeed in what you came here for. I wish those fine young men shout the hell out of you," she curses.

The clerks who work at the Welfare Department arrive at around half past seven, but the place only opens at eight. Before the opening, MaDuma and the others see through the windows how the clerks are answering phones and clearing some paperwork. At the same time, the cleaners are sweeping and mopping the floor. When this is done, which happens exactly at eight, the people are allowed in.

It takes about an hour before MaDuma is close enough to the table to hear clearly what is said.

"Whose children are these?"

"They are mine," answers a young lady.

"Do they have one father?"

"No. They have different fathers."

"Where is the father of this one?" the clerk asks, pointing a finger at the boy of about four years.

"He stays at his home."

"Is he working?"

"No."

"Did he lose a job?"

"No. He has never worked."

"This one?" The clerk looks at the birth certificate in front of him and the child on the back of the young lady. "Where is her father?"

"I don't know."

"Not working again and probably never worked before," the clerk smiles and continues, "Did he ever work?"

The young lady is angry at the clerk's attitude. She tries to control herself for the sake of what she has come for. "When I fell in love with him, he had a spaza shop and earned a fortune from the dagga he sold."

Many people look at the young woman in astonishment.

It is another thirty minutes before MaDuma arrives at the table. She is frightened but tries to control herself. "I have come to register my daughter for the grant."

"Where are you from, Mother?" the clerk shows a strange politeness towards MaDuma.

"I stay at Ndlalidlindoda but I'm not IFP. I voted for the ANC. It's bad nobody saw me."

The young clerk laughs, "You didn't have to tell me that. It makes no difference at all."

"Oh! How can we know? But that is good," MaDuma smiles. The fear she has felt diminishes as she hears the clerk's words. The clerk starts to write and MaDuma interrupts him, "Now tell me, my brother, why does the government not increase this money to at least R300? R100 cannot support a big family of four people."

"This is not for the whole family. It's for your daughter of four years."

"Do you mean," MaDuma is aghast, "do you mean this has to be used for her only? This is crazy. Don't they know we are all hungry? It's not our fault we got older than seven!"

As MaDuma is in town dealing with the Welfare Department, Priest decides to attend the meeting that was announced yesterday, being described as urgent and calling on all the unemployed men and women to attend. Priest leaves his home at quarter to ten, yet the meeting is said to start at nine. He knows that these meetings do not start on time. As he trudges along the street to the courthouse where the meeting is to be held, Priest meditates on his wife's journey. He wishes his wife will be successful. He imagines her waiting in those long queues and feels a tinge of fear. He knows the attitude of those clerks very well. They are rude and unhelpful sometimes. He cannot forget how difficult it was for him to get his ID. He went there four times before he was able to get things sorted out.

Priest arrives at the meeting place at five past ten. There are many people waiting for the meeting to begin. Priest joins those who are seated on the grass. He greets them and allows them to continue with their conversation.

"Our leaders are only concerned about their own well-being." This is a tall man with greying hair. He has been unemployed for eight years now, having lost his job at Narrow-Tex. "They only remember us when it's time for the elections, as it is now," the man with grey hair continues. Priest decides that the man looks older than he actually is.

"Yes, that is what they want from us. Our votes," a young man of about twenty-seven agrees. He is short and dark, with large teeth. He is unable to pronounce some sounds properly, making it a daunting task to listen to him. Priest has heard that the young man could not take his schooling further than Grade Three due to his weak state of mind. He has heard that this young man does not have a fully developed mind because he once ate an *ingobe* – the part of the third stomach of a cow or goat, which the Hadebe clan is prohibited from eating.

"Who is it that actually called this meeting?" Priest asks, to end the silence that has ensued after the weak-minded man has spoken.

"We don't know for sure, but rumour has it that it's the chairman of the Catch-the-Wall Council himself. The one we always hear on the radio talking about how much better they have made our lives," the tall Ndlovu answers. "And they have indeed bettered our lives," he continues, after a pause. "We no longer have to wake up every morning and go to work."

"But we are hungry," another man starts. "In no time we will eat each other like cannibals."

At exactly twenty-five past ten, a Datsun 1400 van arrives at the courthouse. The people look at the car and realise that their host has finally made it. But the car they see discourages them. They were expecting to see a very expensive one.

"We came here for nothing. This man is as poor as we are!"

"Look at him!"

From the Datsun comes a slim, light-complexioned young man of about thirty. As he walks towards the hall where the meeting is to be held, the people continue to speak.

"Look at him. He is thin."

"Too thin for anyone who brings good news."

"He should wear a size twenty-six."

"His car. Even those who were foremen at Blood River Textiles bought better cars than this when they were retrenched. Not this!"

"This is not the man we are waiting for. This one came to attend the meeting like us. He needs a job."

As the people voice their lack of confidence in the man who has just arrived, he calls them in because the meeting is about to begin.

"Oh my God," the grey-haired man complains, "another day wasted. It is truly this thin, poor man who has called us."

"Yes. It's him. There are so many things I could have done at home rather than to come for this," the boy with large teeth adds.

The host of the meeting introduces himself as an employee of the Department of Agriculture, something that alienates him from his audience even more. The people are outraged.

"Why did I come here in the first place?"

"Does this man think we are Afrikaners or what?"

"He is lost. He wanted to go to Mbhavuma's farm."

As the noise continues, the agriculturalist hears and waits for the speakers to finish. When the noise has subsided, he begins, "I may not be rich and big, and I surely do not drive a fancy car. But I think you should listen to what I have to say, now that you are here." He pauses and listens to the quietness that has started.

"The department wants to help people who would like to do farming but do not have the means. We want people to form an organisation and decide on what kind of farming they want to do." The people are listening but become more attentive when they hear the next sentence: "The government will offer funds to start work."

The mention of funds attracts a lot of attention from the people. Many do not like to farm, but it is better than nothing. Here and now it begins to seem like the best option.

The host briefs the people on what they can achieve if they take up farming as a career. "There is a great demand for farm produce in this country. If you take this opportunity, we will ensure that you get access to the market and sell your produce profitably. The government is willing to buy you the land that used to be a game reserve from Place of Power to Upper Gxumani." The agriculturalist realises he has won the hearts of many people.

"I have always liked being a farmer."

"Me too. Farming is my great passion."

"When I was a boy," the grey-haired man starts at length, "my father gave me a cow, which multiplied rapidly. Cows like me very much. It's my late father who brought this smart young man here."

"He is wise indeed. That is why he has no expensive car. He hates beautiful cars, just like me."

"When you've gotten used to him, he is not too thin. He is just medium."

"I think he is on a diet. He is maintaining."

Priest listens and laughs as these people suddenly change their views.

When Priest arrives home from the meeting, his wife has not come back from the Welfare Department. His own journey has been in vain. Not that he expected much. He has heard what the agriculturalist said many a time before. Many people claiming to work for government have come to tell them the same old story that they should form an organisation so that the government will offer them funds to work for themselves.

Now his hope, little of it, is in the journey of his wife. If she manages to secure that R100, at least they will be able to get maize meal. He thinks about the amount of the grant, trying to ascertain its actual worth to the family of four. "If people lived only by eating, this money would still be small. The politicians are just making fools of us, and because we are hungry and pretty much close to being fools, we will do all we can to get that small amount."

Thinking of hunger makes Priest go to the kitchen in search of food, yet he knows there is none. On top of the sky-blue coal stove are three pots, distinguished by their sizes. There is a big, a medium and a small pot. The family normally use the medium and the small pots. Priest opens the medium pot, which is supposed to have pap in it, and realises that it is as clean as he left it. He takes the small one. It is also clean. This time he does not return the lid so soon. He gazes at the pot and the lid alternately, and demands from the pot why it stores no food for him: "What do you think I will eat? Can't you see that I am hungry?" He bellows so loudly that his words echo through the whole house.

After a while Priest leaves the kitchen in haste, as if there is danger lurking. Back in the living room he sees the image of Jesus on the cross that hangs on the wall. Priest climbs on a chair and removes the image. He looks fixedly at it and demands softly, "Why is it that you are only a work of art and you cannot hear us and help us when we are so hungry?"

He goes to seat himself on the sofa, still looking at the image as if he does not want to miss a word of its response. "You cannot even lie to us like the politicians and say you and your Father will come to help us." Priest again allows the image a chance to respond, but it is as lifeless as ever. He then kisses what is supposed to be the head of Jesus.

"I have always loved you despite your being so far away. In fact, I still love you." He fixes his gaze at the image as if it can hear. "But hunger is so powerful that one requires those friends who do not forget him when they have got what they want. You left us here to starve while you live happily with your Father, just like these politicians did when they came to power. The only thing you both want is for us to worship and to support you."

He pauses, as if wondering if he is sure of what he is to say next. "From now on I will not worship or support anyone. I am my own leader and god."

Priest then looks at the wall from where he has removed the image of Jesus. He hurls the image against the wall, exactly where it used to hang, thus breaking it into small pieces.

He stands up abruptly and begins to move up and down in the room, not sure of what he is doing. But what he is doing and what he has done makes him forget that he is hungry. He goes to the bedroom he shares with his wife and takes his tattered priestly garb from the wardrobe. Then he gets the Bible and some Christian and other religious pamphlets. He opens a drawer and takes the four baptism certificates of himself and his family and his own certificate of priesthood and throws all these outside. He then goes back to the room and takes their political party membership cards.

When MaDuma arrives home late in the afternoon, Priest is happily nursing the fire in which he is burning everything in the house that relates to God or politicians. She is very surprised by what she sees, especially the blissful nature of her husband. She demands to know what he is doing, which makes him very happy.

"Getting rid of anything that symbolises our relation to God or the politicians," Priest smiles gently as he speaks.

"I don't understand what you are talking about," MaDuma looks honestly puzzled.

Priest explains, "All our political party membership cards and T-shirts with the politicians' big empty heads and any other things related to politics or the politicians is burning here. All my priest's wear, the Bibles and pamphlets and anything relating to God or His Son are burning here."

That MaDuma is beginning to realise what is going on is evidenced by the change in her expression. "I am sure you did not burn my rosary. Just now I am going into the house to thank God that my journey was successful. When I do that, I am going to hold my rosary in my hand like I did when I prayed for a good journey in the morning."

"It's here," Priest points to the fire. "It is the symbol of our oppression. How long have we lied to ourselves?"

MaDuma is angry with her husband. "I want my God back!" she bellows. She looks fiercely at her husband, as if stating that, if he fails to comply, she will kill him.

However, Priest is oblivious to his wife's anger. "Your God? You have no God."

"You are mad!" she manages to growl through her anger.

Priest is happily tending the subsiding flames. "I have been mad all my life. But I have healed myself now. That is what is good about being your own God," he says, beating his chest.

MaDuma's anger is reduced as she convinces herself that something might be really wrong with her husband's mind. She drags herself inside. She feels some pity for her mentally sick husband, but she is very sorry about her rosary. It has been a part of her life ever since she was a girl. She grew up as a Roman Catholic, and the only thing that mattered to her in the church was singing, because she has a beautiful voice. As she grew up, she showed little or no interest in the God who lives in heaven. She does not care if that God created her and the world she lives in. She does not know Him. Her love and trust is in the rosary, which she can hold and touch and feel. It is close to her. But now it has gone.

19

In the days after the bonfire, Priest wanders aimlessly through the house. His wife and children stay clear of him, thinking he has gone mad. He can no longer visit his friend Sithole as he has always done when he wants to get away from his troubles, and it depresses him to be outside where all he sees is poverty and hunger.

On this day he goes to Sandile's room. As he enters, his attention is taken by some papers on his son's bed. It's a short story called "River of Blood". The one that Sandile spoke to him about – the story that wrote itself. Priest sits on the bed and reads it, page after page. He has just finished the final paragraph when Sandile enters his room.

Priest looks at him with a mixture of anger and disbelief, and says, "Is this how it ends?"

"Yes, Father. I edited it."

"But why? The truth is the truth – we can't change it by ignoring it."

"Of course we can't. But I thought there was too much blood and it might create an impression that violence is the answer."

"What is the answer?"

"I don't know, Father. I do not know."

Once upon a time there was a group of people who lived in a place called Gxumani Maselesele. This name emanated from the saying of these people's language that each and every frog jumps on its own.

Many people in this area were hoping that their new government would improve their lots after they had successfully fought against the government of the foreigners and set up a new democratic government. But when they brought their troubles to the new government, they were told that each and every frog should jump on its own. The new government saw these people as a disturbance to its new rule, saying that these people wanted things for free. After that the people named this area Gxumani Maselesele.

This Gxumani was made up of two very different areas. The one was Canaan, the stronghold of the new government that the people had voted into power. The second one was Ndlalidlindoda, where the voters lived with all their disillusionment.

This story took place a long time ago, but it is still happening today. Perhaps, even tomorrow it will still be happening.

It was on a Friday morning that the Gumede family, with all the families in Ndlalidlindoda, woke up to see their homesteads swarmed by some odd-looking strangers. It was hard to believe that all the people from Spolweni and White Mountain could leave their homes and invade Ndlalidlindoda with everything they owned. But this was what MaDuma saw. She stepped outside the front door and felt her blood race when she noticed that there were about twenty people loitering around in her homestead as if it was theirs. They looked disgusting, ghostly. They looked as if they had been living on the streets for many years. When MaDuma saw how at ease they were as they moved about her grounds, she thought there was only one explanation for it all: it was a dream.

She tried to register everything she saw so that she would be able to tell her husband when she woke up. But when her husband came out of the house and shouted, "*Yeyeni bo!*", she realised she was not dreaming. No! It was not a dream that there were men, women and children loitering inside her home. She was frightened when she noticed that the four men in the group carried sjamboks and did not hide the guns they were carrying at their sides. The women were also armed with axes and bush knives.

"What the hell is going on here?" Priest demanded sternly. "What are you doing here? Have you come to ask for a 'good relation'? If so, why aren't you shouting my clan names?"

Priest tried to sound as fearsome as he could, but the people in his home did not mind his anger. The man who answered him after some two minutes of looking at him harshly was short and dark. He had a round face and Priest thought his mouth was too small for his big head. His name was Phakathi Kwezinja (Among-the-Dogs). He looked like a violent man and would have been a tough guy if he had had enough to eat. In addition to the gun he did not hide, he carried a sparkling spear, which had a big, fearsome stabbing point.

"We are here to eat!" he pointed down with his spear. The other members of the group made some inaudible noise of consent, and Priest first thought of Ethiopia and then of Zimbabwe.

"I don't understand what you are saying!" he waved his hands in the air.

"I said we have come to eat!" the short man said forcibly, and Priest took a step back from him when he saw the spear sparkling.

MaDuma intervened, "If by that you mean you have come to ask for food, we are sorry we do not have it." MaDuma was able to hide her fear. She sounded as though everything was fine. "What we have is not even enough for us."

The mention of some food being available prompted the other members to repeat their noise and Priest decided that they made this noise deliberately to scare them.

"You misunderstood me, Mother. I said we have come to eat, not to ask for food."

Phakathi Kwezinja spoke as coolly as before and this disturbed Priest. It would have been better if Among-the-Dogs' voice had been violent. But he spoke calmly; only his appearance was all violence.

"This is crazy!" MaDuma started. She could no longer hide her anger. "How can you come to us? We are as poor as you are!"

153

"Yes! We are as poor and as black as you are!" Priest supported his wife.

Again, the noise started from the other members of the group and only then was Priest able to place it. It was the sound of the bees. For some reason these people imitated the noise of the bees if they concurred with or disapproved of what was said. In his mind Priest dubbed them Killer Bees.

Priest, like his wife, was confused. It was unfathomable to them why so many pitiful people would come to their home looking like death itself and tell them they have come to eat. What did that mean? As Priest's mind travelled in search of answers, he sent his gaze to his neighbour's home and noticed that there were the same number of people loitering there. He looked at his wife, intending to tell her that MakaNozipho was suffering the same infestation, but he found her eyes were already directed there.

What did one do if something like this happened? What did they want? Priest was about to ask them why they did not go to Canaan, but was interrupted when suddenly they all stood up in silence and began heading straight into the house. At Nozipho's the people were doing the same thing. Were they communicating telepathically? Who were these people?

As if MaDuma had heard his thoughts, she uttered one word that seemed a very possible and unsettling answer: "Satanism!"

For a moment Priest forgot his resolution that he worship no one and said a little prayer: "Oh, Jesus, Son of God, help us!"

But as he heard the Killer Bees helping themselves to the little food that was in the kitchen, he remembered that Satanists eat blood, not food.

MaDuma could take it no longer and decided to go inside her house. She found that one of the older women was serving the little pap they had and had been hoping to eat in the afternoon. Since things had become worse, the family had begun to save their food by eating only once a day and eating only enough to keep them alive.

As she came in, MaSkhwama looked at her with a smile and said, "Don't worry, you will have your share!"

MaDuma realised that she had become a stranger in her house. "We were going to eat that this afternoon. We have nothing else," she said in a sad voice and she sounded as if she was going to cry. What was happening at her home? What was going on at Ndlalidlindoda?

"No one is going to eat while we starve!" MaSkhwama said sternly. "We will all have our share!"

"But why us?" MaDuma said in a voice trembling with tears.

"Oh, don't take it personally. If you haven't noticed, all your neighbours have visitors like us. I assure you that the whole of Phanekeni and Mswane are visited by the same number of people as you see here," MaSkhwama said in a jovial mood, but MaDuma could tell that there was no happiness in it at all.

"Don't say it as if it is a good thing. You are all shameless people of Satan," she replied. As she uttered the last word she hurried outside to her husband and her children, who all looked as if they had never been lonelier in their lives. They stood at the gate, speechless, and MaDuma could not hide her tears watching, as she was, her children scared to death, knowing that she could not help them.

"I am going to call the police!" she tried to reassure them.

"If you want us to die," Priest reproached her.

As they were leaning on the gate, looking west, they heard violent noise coming from Nyandeni's home. It sounded as though the Killer Bees were attacking him. The short man had been a professional athlete and it was possible that he had tried to fight them. Priest and his family listened to the screaming man and his children. Zandi held on tighter to her mother.

Nyandeni came running up the street. Behind him were the younger children of the Killer Bees. Each of them carried a school bag filled with stones. Now they were chasing Nyandeni, stoning him to death.

"Okay!" Priest shouted from his gate. "We get the point! Just don't kill him!"

Priest went out in the direction of Nyandeni to try to help him. As he was going, Sithole came up beside him. "I have good news, Gumede!"

This was the direct opposite of what Priest had expected. There was nothing good about the appearance of the man in front of him. "Well, good for you, because I have nothing but bad news."

"The good news, Gumede, is that as of today I am joining the Watch Tower. I will worship the one and only Son of God. My food will be nothing but the Bible!" Sithole's voice was tired, sad and angry. Priest looked for a smile on his friend's face and found none. Sithole was not joking.

"Why, Job, son of Matshana, what has God done for you that you have changed your belief system so suddenly?" Priest was honestly curious.

"It's not a question of what God has done for me. It's because of what my ancestors have not done for me that I have decided to be a Jehovah's Witness."

"Wow! For a moment I thought you were serious, but you are playing again," Priest smiled dryly as he looked at his friend in astonishment. "That is not a good enough reason to commit yourself to serving God."

"I don't care about that, Gumede! What I do care about is that all this time I have been fooling myself into thinking that my ancestors are protecting me," Sithole felt hot as he spoke, the anger in him immense. "I am particularly disappointed in my great-grandfather, Hlomendlini (Arm-Yourself-in-the-House). How can someone with a name like that and a history of bravery and rudeness let those street people swarm my home? Hhe?" Sithole shouted so forcefully it sounded as if it was Priest's fault.

"But every home here is invaded like yours. It's not like you have bad luck or something," Priest tried to soothe his friend.

"Don't tell me about other homes!" Sithole shouted at Priest. "I am talking about my own." He beat his chest. "Is there a man here in Gxumani who slaughters goats and cattle like I do? Hhe?"

"No," Priest said coolly.

"Now how can you expect me to be content with what happens to the other homesteads? No, Gumede," the anger in Sithole was growing as he spoke.

Priest did not know what to say. How could he tell his friend that religion is not what they have both thought it is? "The invasion of the Killer Bees is as shocking to us as it is to you."

"What is that now?" Sithole was confused.

"I mean these people who have come to rob us of the little food we have. They are Killer Bees because they make the sound of bees and look very much like killers, which they are."

"Hmn! I hate this life! I have never been this confused before. Every time I had a problem I burnt incense and spoke to my ancestors, now I am sure that I have been talking to myself and feeding the poor people of Ndlalidlindoda. Now I don't know what to do. Would you teach me how to pray?"

Priest ignored that question and said to his friend, "You know what I think?"

"How can I know anything if things are like this?"

"Imagine if the Killer Bees came to save us, not to destroy us?"

"What? I talk to you about something serious and you tell me that?"

The Killer Bees stayed and ate in Ndlalidlindoda for about a week. It was on Tuesday the following week that Priest, and all the people of Hunger-Eats-a-Man, were summoned to attend the meeting in an open area bordering the Phanekeni and Mswane sections.

During the week of their stay, the Killer Bees communicated among themselves, as Priest could tell by the coming and going of messengers to his house. They were reporting to MaSkhwama about their progress in the homes they occupied and to take orders from her. Now it was the time for the Killer Bees, whom Priest had heard call themselves The Destitute, to take up their second step of action.

The people Priest and MaDuma found in the open space just above

Yizo-Yizo were so many that Priest felt his scalp tingle. The Killer Bees were armed as before, guarding MaSkhwama, who was speaking through a loudhailer to reach the ears of all who were in attendance.

"I know that those who live here in Ndlalidlindoda are angry with us and think that we are violent and rude." MaSkhwama paused to listen to the response of her audience. There was utter silence. "But I think it may be possible that you will thank us when this is over! Our coming here resulted from the amount of suffering we have gone through. It had reached its limits and we recognised the need to do whatever we could to change our situation."

The people who were listening to MaSkhwama's speech were all seated on the grass. More and more people were arriving, and Priest noticed that some came from as far as Tonga and Place of Power. Everybody looked as grave as if they had lost their loved ones.

"We thought the time has come for the poor to regain their legacy from the rich."

This angered Priest so much that he said his thought aloud. "But why didn't you go to Canaan? You know that we are as poor as you are!"

"I was coming to that, Mr Gumede," MaSkhwama started in her serious tone. "We were aware that to achieve our goal, we needed to get as much support as possible."

She was interrupted by another voice from the crowd. "And what you earned is the direct opposite!"

"I think I should remind you, people of Ndlalidlindoda, that I hate it when someone enters into my mouth. Where I come from, people listen and only speak when they are given a chance."

The response to this was the soft and troubling buzz of the Killer Bees. Priest felt a pang of fear running down his spine.

"Now, where were we?" MaSkhwama said, as a way of calling everyone to the matter at hand. "Oh, I was saying that we came here not because we are oblivious to your economic problems. We came exactly because of them."

The countenances of many people changed as they heard this. They thought MaSkhwama was mocking them. Even Priest couldn't believe it and said to himself, "This woman is a lousy speaker! *Uyibhimbi!*"

"What I mean is that we came to realise the graveness of our situation when we had completely run out of food. Go to any shop at Spolweni or White Mountain and you will find that there is practically nothing. You can have your money but you will die with it because there is nothing!"

MaSkhwama took about twenty minutes explaining to the people of Ndlalidlindoda that they needed them to be in a situation just like theirs so that they too would have nothing to lose and thus have nothing to fear. They, The Destitute, had come to Ndlalidlindoda with their children, not afraid of what could happen to them because they were all dying of hunger anyway. They had come to them first, because they knew that if they were to attack the people of Canaan, they had to be as numerous and as resilient as possible.

"So, on behalf of The Destitute, I would like to say we are sorry to all you people of Ndlalidlindoda and I hope you understand what I have been trying to explain. The question now is whether you are willing to stand up and fight for your lives?"

There was silence as she waited for a response. Those who knew Priest and were seated closer to him looked at him as if saying he should speak for them. Priest, in turn, glanced at his wife and she nodded approval.

"I don't think I have the power to speak for everyone, but as for me, I think it's about time we dealt with these rich pigs who eat everything while we starve. Our language says that the inheritance of the fools is eaten by the clever. I do not think there is anyone here who is a fool!"

There was concurring noise from the people, and the Killer Bees buzzed.

"I do not like violence!" Priest continued after the murmurs and the buzzing had ceased. "But I do believe that there comes a time when the people have to fight for their lives, and I think that time has come for us." Priest paused, took a heavy breath and looked as if deep in thought. Those who knew him realised he was getting into the mood of speaking, and they braced themselves to listen and relish the act. It was always captivating to listen to this man through whom, some believed, God spoke.

"Let me tell you a little story …" He listened again for the audience's reception of this introduction. He sensed that they wanted to hear it. "In the last few weeks I got so hungry that I forsook God! I told myself that God lives up there in heaven and cares for no one but His Son, Jesus. But now I am convinced that the coming of the Killer Bees is the answer to all our prayers."

The people whispered when he mentioned the Killer Bees and laughed when he explained why he had given them that name.

"I think the answer I have found is that God will not do things for us, but will support us if we stand up and do things for ourselves." He suddenly paused, thinking he might have taken more than enough time, so he concluded, "As for me, I join the Killer Bees!"

The people clapped their hands and Priest gave the loudhailer back to MaSkhwama.

After the clapping had subsided, MaSkhwama asked the other people of Ndlalidlindoda if they agreed with Priest, and the answer was an astounding "Yes". She then expressed her gratitude that the people of Ndlalidlindoda were now their colleagues and were willing to invade Canaan with them.

"But I have to warn you that going there will not be as easy as our coming here. The police and soldiers have a way of responding when the interests of the rich are at stake. We have to be prepared for that!"

The Killer Bees, who now included the people of Ndlalidlindoda and those from Tonga and Place of Power, voiced their willingness to fight and die, or get arrested, if it came to that.

"Besides," one man stated, "if we get arrested, we will get food in jail."

The thought of being jailed and fed was not very disagreeable to many people.

It was then decided that The Destitute would make a plan of action. They needed to be careful when dealing with the people of Canaan. Since there were now so many people, it was decided that they form a committee that would be involved in planning the actions of The Destitute because, as the saying goes, too many cooks spoil the broth. This committee comprised forty individuals, twenty men and twenty women. These were elected on merit. Every nominee had to have a record of some courageous deed or be known for a particular talent or for being intelligent. They needed people with different skills to use in this significant and daring adventure. Priest was the first member from Ndlalidlindoda and MaDuma, Belina and MaShandu were also elected. Zodwa wanted to be there but was not nominated.

"This is unfair! I was a member of the Special Five!"

"But you did not deserve to be there in the first place. You were only there because you could run; you have no bravery or intelligence, which is needed now," MaShandu told Zodwa without feeling pity for her. "You want to be in the committee because you like the front seat!"

The Committee of Forty took another week making plans for the Grand March to Canaan. They met daily to share ideas and discuss each group's progress. They had divided themselves into five groups of eight members each, representing all the areas forming part of The Destitute. The main predicament that they had to contend with was the police and soldiers, many of whom lived in Canaan anyway. But they were not afraid of violence – hunger was a bigger threat to their lives.

The arrival of the Killer Bees at Ndlalidlindoda initiated a great deal of excitement and confusion in Canaan. The contempt borne by the Canaanites against the poor people increased when they began to live under the fear of an attack from Ndlalidlindoda. They could not understand why these people were unable to better their lives as they themselves had done. Why were they willing to deplete their strength in destroying other people, instead of using it to help improve themselves? Because they were lazy, silly and jealous. They were too lazy to work for the betterment of their own lives and too stupid to grasp the fact that their strengths would be better employed if they developed them. They were also too jealous to stomach the success of those who worked hard to reach the top.

However, no matter how much the Canaanites theorised about this, the fact still remained that their problem was a practical one. They had title deeds to their houses and sites, and they bought all the food they ate, and toiled for every penny they spent and saved for their children. Yet that in itself could not prevent the jealousy-infected people of Ndlalidlindoda and the Upper Regions from attacking them. They were savages and never thought before they acted. They just wanted to punish the people of Canaan for their success, and the best thing the Canaanites could do was to stay ready for such an attack.

Bongani took it upon himself to ensure that the people of Canaan, including himself, were well protected against the invasion of the Killer Bees and the fools from Hunger-Eats-a-Man. He requested the National Defence Force to come and help the City Police who were already driving up and down the streets of Canaan, in a vain attempt to assure the inhabitants that they had nothing to worry about. The presence of so many police vans and the arrival of brown trucks with many uniformed men and women told everyone in Canaan that something was very wrong.

When the soldiers arrived in Canaan, armed to the teeth as they were, Bongani thought he was supposed to feel safe, but he did not. He looked around Canaan and noticed, as if for the first time, that it was beautiful, modern and urban. It was indeed the land of honey. There were clean parks with well-kept grass and a number of playing grounds for different sports. The roads were in good order and one of them was even called Hadebe Street. Named after him! Every house in Canaan was beautiful and expensive in its own right, although none topped his double-storey. He was still the only one with a double-storey, or The Stairs as it was known.

He had bought himself a Pajero with the money that was allocated for the development of Hunger-Eats-a-Man. It had been enough for the creation of running toilets and tarring all the roads. But Bongani saw that as a waste because the people of Hunger-Eats-a-Man were used to dug-hole toilets and needed only the main road tarred because the tourists used it. Anything more than that would be a waste of time and money, and he would not let that happen.

Bongani realised that he had too much to lose if the people he called the Filthy-Ones invaded Canaan. He began to have sleepless nights. In the little time that he did sleep, he had nightmares in which the Filthy-Ones attacked him and burnt his new Pajero and his double-storey. Nomsa woke him up as he was kicking and screaming, "People of Canaan, run! The fools from Hunger-Eats are here! Beautiful people of Canaan, run for your lives! The Filthy-Ones are here! They are burning my stairs and my Pajero!"

Nobody slept in Canaan or Ndlalidlindoda on the Saturday preceding the Grand March to Canaan – or the Invasion of Canaan, as the Canaanites saw it. The soldiers, police and the people of Canaan expected an attack in the early hours of the morning, but the Killer Bees and the people of Hunger-Eats-a-Man only appeared after nine. All this time the soldiers and the police had waited with their guns ready. But what appeared in Finn Street and Bonner Street was perceived with great shock and horror.

First came the disabled. There were about forty people in wheelchairs and fifty on either one or two crutches, and a number of disabled people with neither wheelchairs nor crutches. Some of these crawled with both their hands and one foot.

As they watched in wonder, on the other side of Canaan there appeared a multitude of children between the ages of seven and fourteen. They were all naked to the waist, showing their bloated stomachs and their bare ribs. They had big heads which contrasted gravely with their lean legs. As they dragged themselves towards the direction of The Stairs, the police and soldiers' attention was drawn away from the cripples and they gazed at the children. It was difficult to estimate their number, each carrying an old school bag and some with plastic bags.

"Stones!" a tall, white man with a beard exclaimed. "They have stones in those bags!"

"Or guns!" another suggested gravely. It was difficult to tell which was which. Were these really children or not? And the cripples? Were they really disabled or were they playing them for fools?

The bulk of the people appeared from the east, from the forest that borders Canaan and the area called The Factories. These were the adults. They charged faster than the children and the cripples. They were also half naked, and women with young babies were feeding them on their bare breasts as they marched. It took some time before the forces of Canaan realised that The Destitute were singing, and even more before they heard that they were singing, "We want to live." They sang their song without force, and the soldiers and police could hear by their voices that these people had gone without food for some time now.

The commander of the Canaan forces was a very dark man in a brown uniform. He rose to the top of the soldiers' truck and shouted through the loudhailer. He had to move around to ensure that all the charging groups heard him. "Stop exactly where you are or we will shoot!"

He tried to sound as threatening as he possibly could, but it was as if nobody heard him except for the other soldiers and policemen. He noticed the children moving faster and singing louder after he had made his announcement. The disabled also did their best to increase their speed and their singing became shriller.

When the disabled had passed Gxumani Community Hall, Bongani noticed that The Destitute were all heading for Hadebe Street.

"They are going to my stairs!" he told the group of confused and cursing Canaanites. "Please stop them! They are going to burn my stairs and pollute my air!" he begged the soldiers, who had their guns ready, but who did nothing. The inhabitants of Canaan were now not only cursing The Destitute, but the police and soldiers too for wasting time instead of shooting the bastards.

Nomsa was looking around for the women of the Grinding Stone. It was hard to tell them apart from the other women. But then suddenly she saw them. It was MaDuma and Zodwa, who were close to each other. They were so emaciated that it was hard for her to identify them.

"MaDuma! Zodwa!" Nomsa shouted. "What is this nonsense? These people you are attacking are your fellow women of the struggle and their children. Don't let these men lead you astray! As a leader of the Grinding Stone, I order you and those men and street children to stop this craziness!"

"These men? These street children?" MaDuma could not believe it. What did this woman take them for? "We are here to fight for our rights as poor people, just like we have been fighting for our rights as women. Sometimes these things do clash!"

Bongani had shouted and begged so much that his voice was now hoarse. When he turned around to watch the buzzing behind him, Priest came forward and called, "I told you we would meet again, PRIN-CI-PAL!"

Bongani moved around as if he was mad and said, "Someone tell me what is the use of having the Defence Force if it does not protect us?"

THE END

Priest finishes reading his son's story and stays in the room for a while. What exactly is this boy saying about them? He has even used their names! But at the end he leaves everything hanging. Why does he not let them beat Bongani and the fat cats of Canaan? But then, Sandile says he did not write it; it wrote itself. What does that mean? After a while Priest goes out. He has a calmness about him that he cannot explain. A good feeling. He knows that this happens to him sometimes. Happiness that comes from no source.

Outside he watches the land and is struck by its beauty. He has not noticed before that spring has come. It has even rained once or twice. Even though the grass is still short – and you can still see the old grass from last season, with its blackness where it was burnt – it is green. His plum tree is blooming. Nature has decorated it with white flowers full of life. He looks up and notices that the firmament is filled with clouds. It will rain today, and he likes it when it rains. Nothing makes him happier than to see the raindrops falling; especially when he is watching it all from the safety of his house.